Short Horror Stories Collections I - III

P.J. Blakey-Novis

Collections I - III

DISCLAIMER: "This is a work of fiction. Names, characters, places and incidents are products of the author's imagination and are used fictitiously. Any resemblance to actual events, locales or persons, living or dead, is entirely coincidental."

Embrace the Darkness and Tunnels copyright © 2017 P. J. Blakey-Novis

The Artist copyright 2018 P.J. Blakey-Novis

All rights reserved.

Cover Design by Red Cape Graphic Design

Www.redcapepublishing.com/red-cape-graphic-design

Contents

Abandonment
Betrayal
Dream Catcher
Embrace the Darkness
Opened Up
The Devil's Pocket Watch
21
The Box
Retribution
Scratches
Trick or Treat
Tunnels
The Artist
The Children of the Deep
The Confessional
Meredith
Unearthed
Wash Away Your Sins

Collections I - III

Collection I:
Embrace the Darkness & Other Stories

ABANDONMENT

"I told you I would never leave you," Marcus said, his eyes red from tears. "I don't understand why you would think that I would." Alice looked at him, sadly. He looked upset, frightened, as he sat on the floor in the corner of their bedroom. "I don't understand what's happening."

"I love you," she told him, with complete and unwavering certainty. "I need to tell you some things about my life; things that I have not told you before, not in any detail anyway."

"You can tell me anything, you know that," Marcus replied, his voice trembling.

"I guess I'm worried about frightening you away, but I need to get it all out. I just can't risk you leaving me. Even so, here it goes." There was a heavy silence as Alice looked Marcus straight in the eye. "They all left. Eventually," she continued. "Some would just grow distant, gradually and over a long period of time. Some were gone in an instant, with the slamming of a door or, in one case, opting for the afterlife. For the thirty years that I've been alive, I have never been able to understand what I was supposed to do with my life. It is only now that I'm starting to take on board what has happened to me, to begin to comprehend why I feel the way I do. And to write my list."

"What list?" Marcus asked from his position upon the floor. His voice was quiet, sensing that something was wrong.

"The list of people who have left me. I don't want you to be on the list, Marcus. That cannot happen." Marcus nodded. "The first person to go had been my own mother (number 1) but as I was only two years old at the time, I really have very little recollection of the incident. Even now, the circumstances around her abandonment of me are unclear, and I do have the sense to know that there was likely to be more to it than what my father had let on. It had been him that had raised me, along with my sister, as you know." Again, Marcus nodded, already vaguely aware of Alice's upbringing. "My father had struggled. And when I was still at primary school my grandmother (number 2 on the list), the only female role model whom I had, committed suicide. It was shocking for everyone, causing arguments and blame to be thrown about the family, but I was too young to make any sense of it, knowing only that my grandma was now gone as well." This was new information for Marcus, and he looked surprised and saddened.

"Sorry," was all he could manage, watching as Alice paced the room.

"It was not until I became a teenager that I thought more about the people missing from my life and, more importantly, why they were not there for me. This is when things had begun to hurt, as though their departure was a direct rejection of me. I mean, if they cared about me, then they would have stuck around, right?

My father had tried his best to raise my sister and me as strong, independent young women but, certainly for me, this had backfired. I became too independent, unreasonably headstrong, clashing with my father and sister more and more often. There was no way of controlling me, no form of discipline that he attempted to use would make any difference. He would hit me over the slightest thing, but this only served to push me further away, so I'd act more recklessly, until one day I left." Alice's voice had risen as she spoke of the physical punishments that her father had dealt out, angry now that he had dared to hit her. Thinking back, Alice couldn't remember what the fight was about on the day that she had left, but she could still see him clearly, standing in the hallway between their living room and kitchen. He had told her that if she didn't like it there, then she should leave. And so, she did.

"This was the point of no return; you see. My pride being too much to think of going back. At sixteen, I found work and a place to live. It was just a room in someone's house, but it was clean, and I was out most of the time. The period of adjustment was fairly short lived, managing to get myself into a healthy routine of eating and keeping my clothes washed. It felt like an adventure, with the freedom to do as I pleased masking the pain of being thrown into the world at too young an age. How old were you when you left home?" Alice asked Marcus, staring at him in a way that unsettled him.

"Erm, eighteen I think, when I went to uni."

"I guess that's quite normal. It must have been nice to leave of your own accord; I felt pushed out. Suddenly, I found that I had a lot of so-called friends, all wanting to stay over as they all still lived with their parents. I would visit my father (number 3 on my list) and sister (number 4) less and less often, feeling more like an outsider with each visit. Can you believe that was fourteen years ago? I can still remember how things felt, how much it hurt. The signs were there, as clear as day for anyone else, but I was oblivious to them." Alice paused for a moment, thinking things over.

"What signs?" Marcus asked.

"That I have some issues," Alice told him, her tone suggesting that it was the most obvious thing in the world.

"I don't think you have issues. You've just been through some things."

"Well, we'll see if you still think that when I get near the end of my story," Alice told him, smiling sadly. "I met a boy whom I thought, certainly at that age, that I really liked, possibly even loved. We were together for a few months, and I would spend all my time with him, not talking to anyone else. However, I would not sleep with him, and that was the problem. Thinking back now, I don't know why I didn't just do it, but perhaps it had been a test to see if he would leave me. Eventually, he did (he's now number 5 on the list), and not just leave, but he started seeing my best friend, who it turned out was more 'up for it'. She is now number 6.

When I was not quite seventeen and, among the terror of hormones and adolescence, I felt alone, angry and lost. I'd reached my lowest point, and it had come suddenly, or at least, it had felt that way. There was nothing to fall back on, nothing to numb the hurt except to take it out on myself. I contemplated suicide but couldn't actually go through with it, so I started to cut myself." Alice stared at Marcus as she told him this, trying to work out what he thought of it. "You don't look surprised," she told him.

"I'm not stupid, Alice. I've seen the scars on your arms and legs."

"Yet you never asked about them." Alice sounded disappointed.

"I figured you'd tell me if you wanted me to know, like you are at the moment." Alice now thought back to those days, how low she had been and how close the end had seemed. Nevertheless, here she was, still alive.

"The next ten years or so feel like they flew by; I moved house often, changed jobs frequently. During nearly all that time, I was not alone, and this now seems strange. Three relationships have filled the last ten years, interspersed with only a matter of months between them and a number of one-night stands. Matthew was the first long-term relationship, my longest at the time, anyway. Eighteen months with a guy a little younger than me, who seemed to worship me. I had moved more than sixty miles away to be with him, and it had been wonderfully exciting. Until it ended, out of the blue, by phone (Matthew is number 7). I never did see him again; I collected my belongings, whilst he was at work, but I still think about him sometimes, even now. He gave me no explanation, and it hurt, of course, but I coped well. I felt stronger at that time; I had a group of friends, and I was old enough to go out to bars and clubs, there were still people around. My mind had wandered back to cutting myself when he had left me, but I managed to resist, for the time being, at least."

"I got dumped after my first long-term relationship," Marcus pointed out. His tone was still friendly enough, but Alice felt as though he were downplaying her sadness. "I know it hurts," he continued. "But you've got me now, I told you I'm sticking around."

"Six months later, I was in another relationship," Alice continued, not acknowledging what Marcus had told her. "This one was to be a real disappointment." Alice thought back to how things had been, how desperate she must have seemed at the start. "We had met at a bar, both drunk, and I had gone home with him. Thinking back now, I wonder how differently my life would have worked out if I just had not given him my number. After the first night he had called me, he wanted to see me again. And again. And again. It was nice to have the attention, and I didn't have much else to do, anyway. That was until I fell pregnant." Now there was a pause. Alice had never mentioned this crucial part of her life to anyone that was still around, but it was out now. Marcus kept a neutral expression in his face, only a slight flicker conveying surprise for just a moment.

"What happened?" he asked, presuming that Alice had opted for an abortion as there was clearly no child with her now.

"If my boyfriend had panicked, lost interest or simply bailed out, then perhaps I would not have kept going, but he was happy about the pregnancy and, therefore, so was I. The feelings I had for him were not strong, but they were, I had hoped, enough to hold things together. We had been with each other for a year when the baby came." A silence hung over them as Marcus tried to make sense of what he was being told. Alice pulled out some photographs from the inside pocket of a long coat which hung in their wardrobe, one that Marcus had never seen her wear. She showed Marcus a picture of a baby, only a few days old by the look of him.

"I thought, seeing him there, lying in that cot, that this was someone who would never leave me. Six weeks after he had been born, we were shopping for tiny coffins (number 8 on my list, my own son)." Alice was struggling to hold back tears now, and Marcus was having the same problem. He had not expected this at all; neither could he imagine the pain that she carried. "That should have been the point at which we went on our separate ways," she told him. "Nevertheless, our grief held us together, neither of us wanting to abandon the other, both sharing in something that no-one else would be able to understand, not ever. The pain that had bound us soon began to tear us apart as we dealt with the loss in different ways. He carried on living his life, going to work, seeing his friends. It was as though he was over it, although I'm sure he wasn't really. He had loved me much more than I loved him, and if I'd stayed, then I think that it would have been enough for him to make it through. Even so, I couldn't stay, I never really had wanted to."

"So, you left him?" Marcus asked.

"I had to. It wouldn't have been fair to stay, but it came hard, never having walked away from anyone in my life. I felt an enormous amount of guilt for abandoning him, the father of my lost child. Nevertheless, I just could not stay, not after what we had been through, wasting the years on someone who I took no pleasure in being with. It was terrifying; I was getting older and scared of being alone, but the constant stabs of deep pain throughout my life had numbed me to feel anything. *Things can't get worse,* I remember telling myself. *So, there's nothing more to be afraid of.* The numbness did not sit well, and I tried to feel something, anything. I needed to find some kind of release. I became more and more distraught as I realized that nothing seemed to work; sleeping around did not make me feel anything, drugs were disappointing, alcohol only made me suicidal."

"I'm so sorry," Marcus told her, tears beginning to run down his cheeks. "You know I'm not going anywhere, though. Right?"

"That's what they've all said," Alice replied, sadly.

"Well, I mean it. I love you."

"You must think I'm crazy?"

"Not at all. I'm just so sorry that you've been through so much. However, it's in the past. We'll be alright."

"I'd understand if you wanted to leave me, I'm a mess!" Alice told him.

"Don't be so silly, I'm here to stay. You and I forever, that's what I told you. Just don't go doing anything stupid! I think it'll help for you to see someone, a professional, I mean. What do you think?"

"It's too late for all that," Alice told him, taking a seat next to him on the floor. "I just need you to decide what you want. You need to choose between staying with me or leaving, because if you are going to go, then please get it over with."

"I've already explained it so many times," Marcus said, trying not to sound irritated. "I want to be with you always; I mean it." Alice began to cry, conflicting emotions fighting in her head. The joy of Marcus promising her forever began clashing with her determination to leave this world, culminating in only one possible course of action.

"Then let's stay together until the end of time," Alice told him, leaning in to kiss him. Passionately and filled with emotion, Marcus kissed her back, absorbed in the moment. So absorbed, in fact, that he did not notice the glimmer of sunlight as it struck the silver blade of the scalpel. The first he knew of its presence was a sharp jab to his neck, his eyes widening as he watched thick spurts of blood spray across Alice's chest.

"Forever," she repeated, opening her wrists up in front of him and cradling his head as the life drained away. She had offered the chance for him to leave, but he wanted to stay. He had made his choice, and now no-one could ever leave her again.

BETRAYAL

There is a thin line between prophecy and witchcraft. The consequences for both could not be farther apart, however. This is something that I learned at a young age. My father was a farmer, still is I presume if he remains alive. My mother married him at just fifteen, almost twenty years his junior, common practice in these times. My father had been married previously but lost his first wife to a plague of sickness, which had swept through the village, taking more than half of the villagers with it. The loss was made doubly tragic as she had been pregnant with his first born but the way that I look at it, if she had survived, then I would not have existed.

Desperately lonely and in need of companionship, my parent's marriage was arranged only a few months later; my father determined to have someone bear him a son whom he could pass the farm on to. Perhaps he has one now; I do not know. It has been over ten years since I have seen him, over ten years since the trial - if you could call it that. My mother fell pregnant soon after they were married, understanding exactly what her role in life was to be. She knew no better and expected no more; content with becoming a farmer's wife and the bearer of his children.

Physically, my mother was not ready for childbirth; her frame too slight to endure the strain that it would put on her. Had she fallen pregnant with one child then perhaps she would have survived, but twins were all too much. My sister was born first, by almost ten minutes, and it was clear to my father, as well as to those assisting in the birth, that all was not well. From what I have been told, which is not a great deal, my mother had lost consciousness by the time they managed to drag me out of her, bleeding profusely from the tears that we had caused. She never awoke, not living long enough to see her seventeenth birthday. My father was inconsolable, having buried two wives and gained no son in exchange for his loss.

As much as he had wanted a son, my father could not bring himself to remarry, unable to face the risk of losing a third wife. He accepted what he saw as his fate, solemnly moving on with his life at the farm, doing his best to raise two daughters alone. I remember him telling us that he did not want to send us off to be married, as was the custom for girls of a certain age. He wanted to prepare us for a life of farming, regardless of what anyone else would think. We looked up to him at that time, and from a very young age, we were taught everything that we would need to know in order to take over when my father was no longer able to tend to the fields himself.

The dreams began when we turned twelve. I say we because my sister had the equivalent dreams, on the same nights. They were virtually identical visions with one crucial difference. I would dream that I had an important destiny, that I would, someday, rise to fame. That I was chosen by a higher power to pass on the prophecies to mortal men. In my dreams, my sister became a force for evil, choosing to live a life of witchcraft and heresy. There was a scene that kept running over, night after night, in which we were both surrounded by a mob of people from the neighbouring villages. The conversation within the dream was muffled, but it resulted in my sister being dragged to a stake, bound and burned alive. As close as we were in the real world, I appeared to feel no remorse in the dream. My sister's dream was identical, except that our roles were reversed, and I was the evil one.

We spent days working within the fields, talking about the dreams each night that we had them. After the first few nights, realizing that they were identical and had occurred simultaneously, we sought the advice of our father. He looked afraid as we explained, in a childlike way, what we had seen. *They are not dreams,* he had told us as we sat around the fire one evening. *They are visions. What you have seen will take place one day, I am sure of it.* He looked sad as he told us this, certain that he was to lose one of his daughters too. *You must stay at the farm, keep yourselves to yourselves. We will just have to see what happens.*

Those dreams had become less frequent, and we had all but forgot about them, by the time we had turned sixteen. My sister and I had had other dreams, of course, but they were nowhere near as vivid. We would dream the same things still, something my father put down to the closeness of our birth. It was only as we got older that we began to notice things, parts of our dreams edging their way into reality. We shared a vision of a storm, more violent than any we had experienced before. A few days later, the farm was hammered with a similar storm, torrential rain flooding the fields, lightning striking the farm equipment. We saw the deformed face of a traveller, who would come by a few weeks in the future looking for shelter. We awoke simultaneously, having envisaged the slaughter of my father's sheep, only to find their carcasses scattered across the field, victims of wolves.

My father played it down, trying to explain away the occurrences, fearful, perhaps, of our power. The vision that changed everything came when we saw the funeral of one of the village elders, a much loved and revered leader. Everyone was gathered around his coffin, leaving flowers and sobbing, his body covered with a white sheet to conceal the gruesome wounds that he had suffered. Personally, I had not considered taking any action about the dream, not knowing what we could possibly have done. My sister, on the other hand, was insistent that we must warn the villagers. *We could save his life!* she urged. My father forbade it. *It's too dangerous if you tell the people, and if something then happens to him, they will blame you! They'll charge you with heresy!*

I accepted my father's ruling and knew better than to disobey him. My sister, however, was far more rebellious than I. Following a terrible argument between my father and my sister, she had waited until we were all asleep before making the trek into the village. She managed to return before either of us could become suspicious, and it was not for another week that we would discover what she had done. It was a hot afternoon when they came, armed with whatever makeshift weapons they had been able to find. As the mob progressed along the dusty track at the edge of my father's land, he sensed that something was wrong, ushering us into the house. From where we sat, hands trembling, peeking through the curtains, we could not make out what was being said - merely that there was an angry discussion taking place.

After a few moments, my father was knocked to the ground, a scythe placed at his throat. Helplessly he watched as they came for us, binding our hands with coarse ropes and marching us into the village. That was the last time that I saw him, lying there, sobbing as we left. I can only assume that he knew what would become our fate and could not bring himself to come and watch. The villagers had clearly been talking about us, working each other up into a frenzy. We were both pelted with rotten fruit and stones as we were led to the village square. That was when everything became clear. As I gazed down on the coffin of the village elder, identical to how he had appeared in my dream, I knew what my sister had done. I felt an anger rise up within me, staring at her, eyes beginning to well up. As good as her intentions may have been, she had been unable to prevent the man's murder.

The villagers formed a circle around us as we stood, a stake having been erected near the centre of the village square. It seemed as though they had already made up their mind. The scene came flooding back to me, just as it had been in the visions of my twelve-year-old self. There was a look of recognition on my sister's face as well, a familiarity with the setting. Nevertheless, her dream had been different; I recalled. There was no way to know yet whose version was accurate. The remaining elders began their speech, citing witchcraft as the reason for our arrest.

You came here, one of you, predicting the murder of our great leader. If you possessed the power to foresee this terrible event, why did you not take steps to prevent it? There was a jeer from the crowd. My sister just looked at me, unsure of how to reply, trying her best not to cry. I remained silent.

Which one of you was it? Speak now or you shall both be charged!

It was me, my sister began. *I brought warning so that it could be avoided. I tried to help you! We both had the same visions; it is not witchcraft. It's a gift!*

A gift? came a voice from the crowd. *We are not to know the future; it is heresy!*

Is it true? the elder asked, looking at me. *You both have these visions?* I will never forget the look on my sister's face as I denied my gift, as I pleaded that I knew nothing of what she spoke, that I was innocent. The look of disappointment and betrayal that she wore etched now into my mind for all eternity. It was my vision that was coming true as they led her to the stake, burning her alive, just as I had foreseen. As hurt as she looked, my sister did not protest, she did not attempt to ensure that I suffered the same fate. As soon as the pyre was lit, I knew though, I finally understood that if one of us were good and one evil, it was not her that should be on that stake.

Too ashamed to return to the farm, I fled across fields and valleys, making my way through the woodland until I came across a ramshackle home which had been deserted for many years. It is from this place that I am now destined to live out my existence alone. The visions still come, more frequently than I would like, but I have no inclination to share them with the world for fear of meeting the same end as my sister did all those years ago. It is a curse that I will have to endure throughout all time, along with the unbearable guilt, taking it to my grave.

DREAM CATCHER

It was brand new technology, an adaptation of those sports watches which monitor how well a person sleeps. It was so completely new, in fact, that they were still in the trial phase. Being keen on both fitness and gadgets, it was only to be expected that Paul had purchased each latest model of watch as they were released. At the bottom of one email from his favourite brand, there was an invitation to take part in the beta-testing phase of the newest design. Paul had signed up to apply without a second thought, after all he was the ideal customer to test such a thing.

The new model was being temporarily referred to as D2V by the manufacturers - Dreams to Visual. From a fitness point of view, it had the same functions that his other watches had had; heart rate, step counter, sleep duration and, of course, time and date. These could all be viewed on the watch's screen and via an app on Paul's smart phone. The key difference, and it was a big one, was the dream function. It was being marketed as being able to record your dreams, with the goal being to establish the possible causes of them. However, the real deal-breaker was the playback function. Recording the pattern of brain activity whilst a person slept, the software could formulate the dream into a visual piece. Essentially, you could watch your dreams when you were awake, like a film.

It was unclear whether or not testers for these samples were chosen at random, or whether Paul's spiel about how he was the perfect candidate had held any sway, but he was chosen as one of five people to take part in the testing phase. The watch was to be dispatched to arrive the following day, and the confirmation email contained a link to the app, from which he could install it on his phone, as the app was not yet publicly available. Paul immediately installed the application, and it was clear that there was still some work to do on its presentation. There was a dashboard, as with the other fitness apps he had used, but currently this only featured the sleep and dream information. As this was the newest technology, it made sense that this should be found to be working as intended before adding the other, simpler, features. From what Paul could tell, the app would record how long he had slept for and any time spent awake or restless, as well as any dream itself. There was a video camera icon on the screen to push when he wished to view his dream from the previous night. Paul found it all hugely intriguing and eagerly awaited delivery.

The next day the watch arrived, looking much the same as any other. It bore the time and date on the rather large face, but all features were disabled bar the dream recording. Alison, Paul's wife tried to show an interest, relieved that he had not spent more money on a device that he did not really need, but she was becoming bored with hearing about how many steps he had taken each day. The dream recording sounded far-fetched to Alison and, despite doubting that it would actually work, she teased him about how she would now know if he had been dreaming about other women. This got Paul's back up, having not found the joke amusing, and he pointed out that he did not remember the last time he had a dream about anything. *What are you testing it for then?* Alison asked him, innocently enough. Paul did not answer, however, deciding to read through the chart that he had been sent with the watch to complete.

It looked fairly straightforward, with boxes to fill in with the date, length of sleeping and basic information that the manufacturers would be able to take from the app anyway. The one box that was extra to the logged information was named 'side effects'. Paul was to write in there if he felt different in any way, whether this was sickness, headaches and so on. *Guess they're just covering themselves,* he thought. The day dragged on and, with the help from a bottle of red wine, Paul finally felt ready to get to sleep. *Let's see what this thing does then.*

The morning arrived with the shriek of his alarm, and Paul sleepily reached across to silence it. He always set his for around an hour before Alison awoke, his intention being to go on a run before she was up. This happened on approximately half of the mornings, which he saw as still quite an achievement. As much as the wine had helped him to sleep, his head ached a little and the thought of leaving the bed was too much at that moment. Glancing at the watch around his wrist, he quickly remembered the dream recorder and decided to test it out before his wife was there looking over his shoulder. *I don't remember dreaming anything,* he thought glumly, expecting there to be nothing to view.

The dashboard on the app showed a video, only three minutes in length. *Well, I suppose it wouldn't run for the same length of time that I was sleeping,* he thought, contemplating how time appears to distort in one's dreams. Taking his earphones from the side of the bed, Paul inserted them into the socket and hit play. The video was jumpy, like a badly edited film. The whole thing appeared to be from his point of view, or at least, someone whom he assumed was himself. He watched as he got into a black car, a large one that he did not recognize. The scene jumped to him walking through an empty city at night, then through a green door at the side of an unmarked building. Suddenly, Paul found himself in some sort of underground nightclub, possibly the interior of the building he had just entered, perhaps somewhere else entirely. It looked similar to something he had seen in a film recently and assumed that this was where the thought had originated.

As the video continued, Paul saw himself approach the bar and the scenes merged into one blurry tale. He was downing shots of an amber liquid, flashing lights cutting through the darkness inside the room to illuminate the crowd. Suddenly, two women appeared beside him, looking as though they were talking to him, but he could not hear them over the music. Dressed in tight leather and with multiple piercings, they began kissing each other as Paul stared on and then, for an unknown reason, they wrote a telephone number on a book of matches bearing the club's logo of an upside-down cross with an eye above it. It was as one of the women, the one with the large spider tattoo on her neck, handed him the number, the video ended. *Bloody alarm clock!* Paul thought.

He struggled to understand the video and, apart from being glad that Alison had not watched it, he did not know what to think. He certainly did not remember having that dream, but he had read somewhere that we dream every night, usually completely forgetting it, by the time we awaken. While the dream was fresh on his mind, Paul decided to fill out the feedback sheet with the data and get himself ready for the day, having enjoyed the video and becoming more intrigued to see what tomorrow's would look like.

Alison was not working that day and had barely risen when Paul was ready to leave for work. He bid her good-bye before she had chance to ask about any dreams and made his way out to his car only to find himself blocked in. The car was parked outside their house, as usual, but he had left it with the rear bumper close to the front of the one behind. Some inconsiderate sod had parked in front of his, in the identical fashion that he had. Most of the cars on their street were the same ones each day, and he had a good idea of who owned which. This one was different though; it looked out of place but strangely familiar. *Maybe someone bought a new car?* he wondered, seeing that he would not get out of the space with the big, black 4x4 in the way. The car behind belonged to the lady who lived next door, so he knocked for her, hoping that she would be able to move it for him. After a few attempts, there still came no answer, and he unhappily wandered along to the nearest bus stop, calling his workplace to forewarn them of his inevitable lateness.

The bus journey felt as though it was taking much longer than usual, something that often happens when one is in a hurry. It was the same route as he had taken many times before, in the days prior to owning the car, but there were parts that looked different somehow. *I haven't taken a bus for a while,* he thought. *I'm sure it's nothing.* It was only when he stood up to get off the bus that he felt a hand grab his arm. Turning suddenly, he saw an elderly man holding on to him.

"You dropped this," he told Paul, opening his hand slowly. Paul's eyes widened as he looked at the black match book, cross and eye logo featured on the front of it. Quickly, Paul snatched it from the man and stuffed it into his pocket without so much as a thank you. It was too much to process, making no sense at all. Had he actually dropped it? If so, how did he come to even have it? Heading down a narrow walkway as a short cut to the office, he paused to open the matches. Inside was a telephone number, just as he had seen in the video. He decided, as he was already late for work, to replay the footage and try to make sense of it. *The car!* Paul saw that the car from his dream looked almost identical to the one outside his house. The matches were also the same. *But where was this club? And those women?!*

Trying not to panic, Paul asked around about nightclubs, as casually as he could manage. It didn't come naturally for him, his years of clubbing having long since passed and the gothic, metal scene was not one with which his co-workers would associate him with. No-one seemed to know of the place he was describing, having told them that it was somewhere Alison had suggested that they go one evening. The day moved slowly, even after being an hour late to work. The only contact he had had from Alison was a text asking him why he had not taken the car. Paul told her that it had been blocked in by 'some idiot with a 4x4' and that next door were not home. Apparently, the car was gone by the time Alison had looked outside.

Paul chose not to mention the dream video or the matches as he was unable to explain of it. There was a strong temptation to call the number on the matches but, as foolish at it sounded, he was scared to. He did, however, decide to write on the feedback form about these strange occurrences in the 'side effects' column. As impossible as they seemed, there had to be some kind of connection. Before bed on that second night, Paul decided to watch the video one more time in the hope that his dream would continue from where it had left off. *Perhaps something about the club's location will be revealed? Maybe something to identify the women?*

When morning came, once again his sleep interrupted by his alarm, there was another video. This was a longer one, nearer to five minutes. Whether or not it continued on from the previous footage was impossible to say, the timeline in dreams not being as linear as in real life. There were similarities between the two clips, however, especially the 'feel' of them. If they had been movies, they would have looked as though they had had the same director. The second dream was more surreal than the first and featured Paul apparently stumbling across some kind of secret society preparing for a ritual of sorts. It was, again, very jumpy and Paul saw winding tunnels, torches of fire adorning the walls. There was a line of people passing him as he wandered along them, all in red gowns with their hoods up. No one was speaking. As soon as the last person passed him Paul turned to join the end of the procession, looking down to see that he too was wearing a red gown. He followed them through to a large chamber, hundreds of candles illuminating it. A huge stone pentacle was embedded into the rock beneath his feet as he gazed upon a marble table that was by now encircled by the other people. On the table was a woman, fully nude, face down. Her ankles and wrists were tied to poles, spreading them as far as she could manage. From where Paul stood, her head was farthest from him, affording him a rather explicit view.

Terrified at what appeared to be about to happen, Paul turned to try and leave. His path was blocked, however, by a female figure. The red hood masked most of the features on her face, only a large tattoo of a spider being visible on her neck. It was at this moment of finding some familiarity that his alarm clock must dragged him back to reality, and the video ended suddenly. *This is fucking weird,* he thought, not having the slightest memory of any dream, especially ones like these. Today Paul did feel sick, which he put down to the general state of confusion that he was in. Nevertheless, once he had had the idea that he should call work and take a day off; it was decided. Alison would be leaving within an hour or so and then he could try to get to the bottom of what was happening. Once the bathroom was free, Paul opted to take an excessively long shower, hoping that his wife would not think of asking if the watch had captured any dreams yet. He told her that he was feeling a bit funny and not going to work. She looked at him suspiciously, knowing full well that he was fine and wondering what he was up to. Alison chose to say nothing and, after giving him a peck on the forehead, left the house to go to work.

Time to man up, Paul thought as he began to dial the number from the book of matches. There was no answer, but it went to an answering service, a woman's voice telling him to leave a message, and she *might* get back to him. He chose not to, unable to think of anything to say. He certainly couldn't think of anything believable anyway. Wandering around the house in just his towel, Paul tried to decide what he should do. He thought about calling the people who had sent him the watch but doubted they would have anything useful to say; they'd probably think he was insane if anything. He regretted not taking the number plate of the 4x4 and now had no way to try to follow up on that potential clue. Turning to the Internet for help, Paul began searching for clubs that sounded similar to the one he had seen. There were none anywhere near to wear he lived, the nearest rock and metal clubs being more than an hour away. He had no luck finding the logo either and started to read up on sacrificial rituals, desperate to find a solid link. *Of course, it could just be constructed from my mind, dreaming something doesn't make it real,* he told himself, trying to ignore the fact that the matches on his kitchen table were indeed very much existent.

The information that he found online was tedious and very general, mostly referring to suspected rituals carried out by various groups, but with nothing confirmed as being accurate. There were no known groups which wore red gowns and sacrificed women, assuming that was their intention, above the symbol of the pentacle. After two mugs of coffee and no real progress, Paul made his way back upstairs to get dressed. Opening his wardrobe, he almost missed it at first, pulling a T-shirt off of a hanger. Changing his mind on the choice of clothing, he went to hang it back up when he saw it. It would be more accurate to say he felt it before actually laying eyes on it, the softness standing out as unfamiliar. Hands beginning to tremble, Paul slowly removed the red, hooded gown from his wardrobe, the sickness that he had felt earlier becoming a full-on wave of nausea.

Paul threw the gown on to his bed, along with the matches, and stared at them. To begin with he felt confused, muddled. Now he felt terrified, more so than he had ever been before. *It has to be a prank,* he told himself, hopefully. *But it's not fucking funny if someone is coming in my house!* Angrily, Paul redialled the number from the matches and this time, left a message. *I don't know what's going on, but it needs to stop now. You've had your fun.* Having been unable to shout at an actual person, Paul still felt on edge and chose to call the manufacturers of the watch. The customer service adviser did not sound remotely concerned or surprised by what Paul told her. She explained patiently that the software had created a visual record of his dreams, and it was perfectly normal to see things from these dreams when awake, but that these were coincidences. After all, she had said, there are probably thousands of black 4x4s. Paul tried to explain, as calmly as he could, that the gown which had appeared in his wardrobe was not there before. He only saw it in the dream. *Perhaps it's your wife's and you didn't know she had it,* was all he was told. Accepting that he was getting nowhere he finished the call without saying good-bye.

Soon realizing that Paul would know nothing further until the watch had recorded some more footage, he became desperate for the night to come. It was barely lunchtime and he felt helpless as he waited, frightened of what was to come next. There were still at least six or seven hours until Alison would be home, and then it came to him, an idea that was definitely worth a try. A few months ago, after a bout of quite severe depression, Alison had been prescribed temazepam. Paul recalled how they would render Alison asleep within half an hour, sending her off for a good four to five hours if she only took one. He reasoned that, as he was supposed to be ill anyway, it wouldn't seem too strange should he be in bed when she returns and grabbing a bottle of water from the fridge, he decided to take two of the pills and get into bed.

Taking one pill would have been more sensible it seemed, nine hours having passed whilst Paul slept. He awoke groggy, a little confused from sleeping during the daytime. Once he saw how long he had been out for he made his way downstairs to find his wife, but she was not there. Glancing out of the living room window, he could not see her car parked anywhere nearby either. *Strange,* he thought and went back upstairs to get his phone. Seeing no messages from his wife to explain her absence, he prepared himself to view the latest dream footage, scared of what he would see.

The dream had continued, exactly from the point at which the last had ended. Paul stood in the red robe, gazing at the face of the woman he had met in the bar. No one spoke; the only sound within the room was the stifled murmurs of the woman tied to the table. Paul turned back to look at the naked victim, watching her writhe about in an attempt to get free. Her head was covered by a mask of some sort, similar to the kind worn at nineteenth-century dances. He watched as someone broke from the circle and approached the victim, something glowing in their hand. It was only as they rose it into the air that Paul saw that it was a branding iron. Helplessly he looked on as the upturned cross and the all-seeing eye were burnt into the woman's back. Paul quickly turned to leave, attempting to overpower the tattooed woman, but to no avail.

Despite there being no conversation, something propelled him to act. It was a form of acceptance, as though he knew what was expected of him, and he felt that the consequence for refusing far outweighed the terrible act that he was to perform. Sitting on his bed, Paul watched as he moved forward in the video, standing directly behind the bound woman. The film was jumpy again, so it was unclear as to where the knife had come from, but it was now in his hand, and he had to do as requested. Raising the blade into the air with both hands around the handle, he plunged it into the woman's back repeatedly. He heard a cracking sound as it hit bone, sticky scarlet spurts emanating from the gashes he was leaving on her. Viciously, infinitely more so than he could imagine himself being capable of, he kept stabbing, repeatedly, until all he could see was red. As he looked around at the others who had watched him, they began to clap. The applause grew and grew, echoing from the cavern walls. Then it ended, just like that.

After finding the matches and now the gown, it should not have been too surprising when he found something else, which did not belong. Only this time, it sort of did. The knife was his, from the block in the kitchen. The blood, however, could have been anyone's. Fear set in once again, dreading what had happened, terrified of what would be coming next. *Would this all stop if I just take the watch off?* he wondered. Unable to think of anything else to try, he removed the watch and attempted to call his wife. The call went straight to voice mail. It was too late to call her workplace, so he would have to wait. Being alone and frightened was not good, and he hoped that Alison would be back soon so that he could tell her what was going on, perhaps she could help somehow.

The sound of the doorbell interrupted his train of thought and, without considering why Alison would not have just let herself in, he headed to answer, relieved to have her home. The four police officers at his door came as a shock, fearing that something had happened to his wife. With little explanation, Paul was cuffed and led to a waiting police car while the other officers made their way into his home. The conviction was solid; the police having found the knife covered in Alison's blood as well as video footage of the ceremony itself. She was found down an alleyway, outside a green door. Apart from a mask, she was fully nude and, among the seventy-four stab wounds to her back, there were the remnants of some satanic symbol burnt into her skin. There were traces of hair and fibres from both himself, and Alison discovered in the back of a black 4x4 hire car, registered under his name. His version of what had happened was laughed away, no one believing in a dream catching watch or any of the other oddness surrounding the case. The more he protested his innocence, the less anything made sense and Paul was deemed to be delusional, not to mention extremely dangerous. He was never to be released from the psychiatric facility and would spend the rest of his days in his own room, the only human interaction coming when his meals were delivered by the pretty girl with the spider tattoo on her neck.

EMBRACE THE DARKNESS

I was around seven or eight when I first had a nightmare. At least, that was the initial one which was vivid enough that I can still recall it. It was short, not a lot of detail being provided in my mind. I saw myself lying upon the bed in my small room and there, in the farthest corner, between the top of the wall and the ceiling, was the creature. It had formed a kind of nest, strings of white hanging from the ceiling as it nestled there, web-like entrails surrounding its dark form. In my dream, I could not see it properly. It appeared just as a shape, but the terror which I felt that night is something that I remember well. I did not sleep in my own bedroom for a number of weeks after that night.

When I was fourteen, I awoke in the early hours of the morning, screaming. My sleep had been interrupted by another nightmare, a continuation from the one I had had all those years previously. I was still sleeping in the same bedroom. We had resided at the house all my life, only my bed was on the opposite side of the room at this point. The monster, however, was back in its original spot, now appearing directly above me and this time it had begun to move. I recall the dream as clearly as I do the previous one. I remember, in my dream state, gazing up at the creature and thinking, *'That's the same monster from my dream before!'* It was a feeling of wonderment, rather than fear, to begin with. That was until it started to shift, an almost human-like face unfurling, jet black in its entirety except for two pupil-less, perfectly round, white eyes. As the terrifying face began to push against the web which it had created for itself, I screamed, waking from the nightmare as I sat upright in bed.

My fourteen-year-old-self was more able to accept that it had only been a nightmare, but I still felt uneasy each night, desperately trying to think about other things before sleep took me. No sooner had I managed to banish the dream from my mind, then I had another one, yet again the same. It was only the briefest moment, that awful face continuing to press against the web as if it were trying to come closer to me, but the level of terror that I felt was enough to begin affecting me during my waking hours. I would see the creature in a whole host of places, more and more often as the weeks went by. My family thought that I was suffering from arachnophobia at one point due to the way that I would recoil from the sight of a spider on its web. Shadows in the corners of rooms would take the form of that face, nowhere felt safe.

Between the ages of fifteen and twenty, it haunted me. I saw it almost daily, regardless of where I was it would find a way to reveal its face. The constant torment had serious repercussions for my mental wellbeing, resulting in a dependency on anti-anxiety medication as well as, on the insistence of my doctor, some experimentation with anti-psychotics. I blamed my childhood bedroom. I longed to sleep anywhere but there and so, at the age of sixteen, I left. My family understood, to a point, my reasoning, but they were frightened for me. It was not as though they believed that there was anything dangerous about the dream itself, of course, but they could see how my mental health was deteriorating so rapidly.

I found a small room not far from home, renting from a man who was mostly away on business, thus leaving the whole house to me. I thought it would be perfect; I thought I would be safe there. Nevertheless, the dreams became more regular still, each visualization bringing the creatures cracked, blackened face closer to mine. I became dangerously close to the edge of existence, feeling the immense pull of both anxiety and depression. My mind was a constant battle between being too frightened to leave the house and too afraid to stay in it. I never knew if I wanted to be alone, or if I needed company, I found it difficult to distinguish between what was real and what was not.

As much as I struggled, I managed to hold down a job, and I managed to control, what the doctor had called, my symptoms. There were specific places which I had to avoid, such as dark alleyways and suspicious-looking marks along the sides of buildings, and this caused me to take the long way to and from work each day. I did not dare to tell my colleagues, most of whom I would drink with after work, for fear that they would ridicule me, and so I suffered my burden for months on end, positive that one night the creature would finally reach me.

In my dreams, I was always back in the bedroom at my family home, the dream being virtually identical each horrific time that it came to me. It had been devastating that my plan to live elsewhere had not helped and now, regardless of anything, that thing was etched so deeply into my mind that it had become a part of me. I wanted it to go, to leave me in peace, but it would not. I searched for help, sure that there must be a way of erasing the memory, but there was nothing. All I could do was embrace it, fight the feeling of gut-wrenching dread and not pay it any attention. This was what I had decided and, as hard as it was, I began to face my fear. I started to take the more direct route to work, music blasting in my ears, eyes darting anywhere except where the shadows would lie. I'd stay awake for much longer than was healthy, pushing myself to the extreme until even the mix of caffeine and recreational drugs could not keep sleep at bay.

The dreams slowly started to subside, sleep having been replaced with a deeper level of unconsciousness, and I felt as though I was finally winning. That was how it had seemed to me, anyway. From the outside, I was a mess, sleeping only two or three hours each night, dependent on amphetamines, rarely eating. My parents were worried, making their disapproval of me ever so clear, and I reacted in the easiest way that I could; I stopped seeing them. I chose to do that rather than risk the nightmares returning. My friends and colleagues did not seem to see me as the disaster that my parents described me as, possibly because they were all a mess in their own ways. We were all young, we all wanted to the same kind of excitement and we all felt a need for escape.

On the approach to my twenty-first birthday, someone suggested we went camping, a group of us, to some woodland not far from home. It was always deserted, I was told. It could be fun, they all said. My anxiety kicked in at the thought of being in the woods, surrounded by that pitch black, enveloping darkness. I told them that I would think about it, tried to brush it off as 'camping not really being my thing'. However, they had made the decision, and they insisted that it would be great. There would be drinks, there would be drugs, so potentially I could stay awake all night. I'd have plenty of company; I would be safe. Peer pressure, being the thing that it is, gave me little choice when the day came around and so, with just a bag of essentials and a large torch, I made my way out with five others.

I was very self-aware; I had learned what triggered the fears, and I knew how to manage them to the best of my ability. I was also very keen on drugs but, for the sake of trying to cling to my last strands of sanity, I had avoided any hallucinogens. It sounded like an insane idea for me to try anything like that, I was seeing things far too often without the help of drugs. This is the reason I refused the mushrooms that night. Even so, I did not explain why. And this is the reason my friends gave me them anyway, without my knowledge. From what I had been told previously, hallucinations are all well and good provided you know that you've taken something. If you have no way of knowing that it is the drugs, rather than reality, things become much more sinister. Especially if your mind is already packed full of terrifying images.

We made a fire, sitting around it passing a couple of bottles of cheap scotch back and forth. I drank it, preferring that to the bloating, sleep-inducing effects of beer. I let the cannabis pass me, knowing from previous experiences that it would knock me out and, with a couple of pills inside me, avoiding looking into the darkness, I began to relax. One of the girls announced that she was going to get some snacks and wandered off to the pile of bags and coats that we had slung at the foot of a huge tree. The drugs had completely destroyed my appetite, and I could not face food, but as I tried to decline, she smiled so sweetly at me. Foolishly, I thought she was interested in me, coming back to the group with only a handful of pastry bites. She popped one in her mouth and held one up for me, her fingers running across my lips, my mouth opening. Two were all that I could manage and no sooner had I swallowed them then the girl began laughing. She made no explanation as to what had amused her so much and I, mistakenly, put it down to her drunkenness.

I was unaware of the hour, but it was late enough to be dark during the summertime, certainly approaching midnight at least. The cover of the trees and the remote location had created an eerie shadiness as night enveloped our merry group. I had lost track of the conversation, it having been centred around some band I had not heard of, and my eyes had begun to wander towards the trees. The clearing in which we were sat was small, aside from a little trail along which we had wandered, we were now completely surrounded by woodland, and I was starting to feel anxious.

The nearest trunks were only a few metres away from me, and I could detect their form as they stood, towering above us menacingly. Beyond the trunks was an inky blackness, nothing else being visible. Almost nothing. As I looked over the shoulder of the person sat opposite me, I noticed two white circles, a few feet from the ground, perfectly spherical and close enough to one another to be eyes. Pupil-less eyes. I took a double take, trying to convince myself that it was just my mind playing tricks on me, that I was safe despite the threatening feel of my surroundings. On the second look, I could not see them, but then they were back, this time a few feet to the left of where they had been previously.

A look of fear must have been noticeable as my friends started to ask if I was alright, through little giggles and knowing smiles. I told them what I'd seen and, as amusing as they were finding my sense of dread, one of them confessed to the mushrooms. I was angry but tried to conceal it, terrified of embarrassing myself but equally convinced that what I had seen was real. If I was to be afraid, then so should they, as reprisal for their cruel prank. I began to talk about my dreams, the things that I had seen, theatrically telling the scary story around the campfire. I described the blackened face of my visitor, the bizarre form that it seemed to take, the sticky, imprisoning web that it formed.

Everyone listened intently, enjoying the tale. The guys laughed it off but the girls, more easily frightened, began scouring the tree line for anything out of place. In order to prove his bravery, or to reassure the girls, and myself that there was nothing to fear, the young man opposite me stood up and announced that he needed to take a piss and would be back soon. Unless the white-eyed monster gets me, he told us with a chuckle. We heard the crack of brittle twigs as he made his way into the darkness, the rest of us waiting in total silence for the sound of his return. He had not ventured far, and we could hear the splash of urine as it sprayed against a tree. Then we heard nothing. No more rustling leaves, no more crunching footsteps. Only silence.

Convinced that he was playing a prank on us, we began a new conversation, certain that he would get bored and reappear shortly. After a good ten minutes or so there was still no sign, and it became clear that we would need to investigate, something that not one of us was willing to do alone. My heart was racing, the terror, combined with the drugs, now pushing it to its limit. The girls began to call out for our missing friend, becoming angry that it could be a joke. It only took a few steps into the woodland before someone screamed. The rest of us, unable to see the gruesome spectacle, raced to get back to the clearing.

I had been at the back of our group and so was the first one to reach the fire. I turned around to see that we were now half the number we had been when we had arrived, just myself and two girls stood in shock. We called to the others to no avail but did not have the courage needed to return to the darkness to look for them. All we could hope to do was to grab our belongings and run, to try to find help. No sooner had they bent down to pick up our bags, then I saw it again, the eyes staring from the darkness. It all happened so quickly, the speed at which it claimed its prize was unexpected. In a matter of seconds, the creature had appeared, long, thin legs propelling it rapidly in circles around the tree that our bags were strewn beside. The white, tangled, sticky web sprayed from the end of its short, almost birdlike arms and after the shortest moment, it had bolted back into the night.

Silence fell once more, the girls now secured against the trunk of the tree by the creature's web. It had engulfed them with such force that they had been bent and twisted, limbs contorted at angles which were not usually possible, one of their heads suddenly facing the wrong way. If they had survived the envelopment, then suffocation would have surely taken them, but I had no doubt that they had met a quick, albeit horrific, demise.

I could not run, fear having fixed me to the spot, and I now knew that this is what had been waiting for me, it had been on its way since that first dream as a child. I stood beside the fire with my eyes closed and took a large gulp from the whiskey bottle. Embrace the darkness, I told myself. It seemed inevitable. I waited but there was nothing. I knew that the horrors which I had just seen would drive me over the edge, and I saw no way to go on living after this. I did not want to be the sole survivor, to have to face my fears day in and day out once again. Eventually, I opened my eyes, wondering why the beast had left me standing, only to meet the gaze of two white circles. The black, cracked face was inches from mine, a crooked smile having appeared revealing equally sooty teeth.

Simultaneously, the creature and I raised our arms and as the web began to fly from it, I held the rough, jet black skin in an embrace. I held it in my arms, feeling the tightening of the restraints as they bound us together, my lungs beginning to struggle for air. The monster and I became as one, cocooned with each other in inescapable bondage. I felt myself slip from consciousness, the only sound being the crack of my bones as I was crushed against the blackness of my nightmare. After years of torment, terror in every waking and sleeping moment, the creature had finally taken me. Even so, I had also taken it, and now we were both complete.

OPENED UP

The doctor had seemed more concerned about the lump than I had, having just shown it to her on the off chance that it warranted taking action. A year, I told her. That was how long it had been noticeable, protruding from the top of my foot as though a golf ball had been stitched beneath the skin. It did not hurt, I explained, which is why I virtually ignored it all this time. Recently, however, there had been a little discomfort when wearing shoes, as if the increased mass of my foot was now too much to fit inside my favourite brogues.

"We will need to do some tests," she told me, her eyes meeting mine as she tried to portray the seriousness of the situation.

"OK," I told her. "So, what is it?"

"The chances are that it is harmless, most likely a ganglion cyst, and will have to be removed. Nevertheless, we need to arrange an ultrasound scan, to rule out anything more serious." *Cancer,* I realized, the thought having not entered my head thus far. I did my best over the next few days to keep any panic from my mind, having read online that the chances of it being a cancerous growth were less than two in one hundred. Even so, the doctors were incredibly efficient, and I received an appointment for the ultrasound within a week.

"Looks like a cyst," I was told as an implement was run across my bare foot, squelching through the cold jelly.

"It looks like a cyst, or it is one? Like, for definite," I asked, needing some clarification.

"It looks like a cyst," the ultrasound nurse repeated, this time taking his eyes from the monitor to look at me. "I would bet that it is a cyst. That said, there have been times that we've been wrong and not known until the surgeon starts taking it off. Either way, it's got to go." I was told to expect an appointment for surgery very soon, most likely at a private facility due to the longer waiting lists at public hospitals.

Ten days later, I found myself sat in the waiting area of a small private hospital, on the surgery list of a Mr. Yambus. The morning, they told me. That was as specific as they could be, but I would be one golf ball sized lump lighter by midday. Due to the anesthetic, I was not to eat that day, and as I sat as patiently as I could, my stomach began to rumble. After almost four hours of pacing the waiting room and watching all the other patients disappear to theatre, I went to enquire about the holdup.

"Mr. Yambus is on his lunch break now; I'm afraid," the crow-faced receptionist told me.

"I'm supposed to be having an operation this morning. What time will it be then?"

"Take a seat, I'll find out." With that, the receptionist left her station and scurried away down the corridor. This is the point at which I should have felt that something was amiss, her absence for the next forty-five minutes being a good indicator. Three-quarters of an hour I spent sat in that room alone, no other patients, no visitors and, now, not even the receptionist. The only time I stood from my chair was to visit the toilet which was at one end of the room. If I had needed to venture further maybe I would have seen that all was not as it should have been. If I had attempted to go back out to the street, then I may well have panicked upon finding the large glass doors of the main entrance now locked. I remained blissfully unaware, only mildly irritated by the delay, more distraught by the lack of food.

Despite the strangeness of the situation, I played the part of the model patient, waiting as instructed. Finally, the receptionist returned. Physically, she appeared the same but there was something unfamiliar about her. I could not put my finger on it, only a sense that she had returned and was now different. Her voice was slower than before, her eyes not quite looking at me as she spoke.

"Sorry for the delay," she mumbled; her gaze just passing over my left shoulder. "The doctor is ready for you now. Follow me." She led me along the corridor from which she had appeared, arriving at a staircase to my left. I glanced up the stairs ahead of me and saw that the next floor was in darkness. As we began to ascend the stairs, the light fading, I had to ask the reason.

"Is there something wrong with the lights up here?"

"Not that I am aware of," she replied. "But it's an old building. It seems a little dim upstairs, I'm afraid." *A little dim!* I thought. *It's almost completely black!* At the top of the stairs, we passed through a doorway into a narrow corridor with drab, red carpets. The walls were painted in the repossessed house colour of magnolia with a hideous burgundy, floral border wallpapered along them. Damp patches appeared above the skirting boards, and all was eerily silent.

"This is your room," I was told, the words sounding almost robotic as they slowly struck my ears. "Get into the gown and I will be back soon."

I pushed to open the door to the private room, expecting the same level of darkness but my eyes were in for a shock. There was no issue with the lighting inside, the brilliance of it causing my pupils to retract suddenly. Once inside, I closed the door and looked around. It was spotlessly clean, as a hospital room should be, but in stark contrast to the corridor outside. There was a private bathroom and a hospital bed, a machine for taking observations, even a television fixed against the wall. The uneasy experience outside soon dissipated once inside, and I stripped out of my clothes, unsure whether or not to leave my underwear on beneath the gown that had been provided. I decided that, as the surgery was to be on my foot, there was no need for me to expose everything to the medical staff.

A few minutes later, as I struggled to drag the surgical stocking across my good foot, the receptionist returned and invited me to follow her once again, into the darkness of the corridor. We walked slowly through the darkness, my eyes following the line of wallpaper on either side of me. It was unexpectedly long, the hallway, and it was only as I started to feel we had walked further than I had anticipated, that I began to notice there had been no breaks in the wallpaper. No breaks and, therefore, no other doors which could have led to other rooms. As I weighed up whether or not to enquire about this oddity, the receptionist stopped suddenly. Slowly, she raised an arm, pointing ahead into the blackness.

"Take the lift down to level B, someone will meet you there." I could see no lift, or anything else up ahead, but I made my way cautiously regardless. *B?* I muttered, to myself. *As in basement?* I came across the shiny surface of the lift door and was relieved to find the inside of it was as brightly lit as my room had been. There was a choice of three buttons to press, 1, G and B. It was obvious that I was currently on level one, the first floor and, as unsettling as it sounded, I had to accept that level B was indeed the basement. In the short moments that the lift was in motion, I feared that I might step out into some horrific scene, some insane surgeon strapping patients to a metal table in the middle of a poorly lit room. This was not, however, the case.

I was greeted by a young woman as the lift doors parted. She spoke in broken English as she explained that she was the anesthetist and led me to a small room next door to the lift shaft.

"Do you have allergies?" she asked, her accent sounding as though she may be Polish, or Russian, perhaps. I told her that I did not have allergies, and she indicated to the bed, which I climbed upon, doing my best to keep my underwear covered.

"You feel a little prick," she told me, holding a long, thin syringe in one hand. My immature streak showed itself for a second as I let a little smile pass my lips at the words 'little prick'. As it happened, it was a rather sizable prick as I felt the needle pierce a substantial vein on the top of my left hand.

"Count backwards from ten," she ordered, placing a mask across my nose and mouth. "Out loud."

"Ten, nine, eight, seven..." and then I must have been gone. I could not say how long I was out for, only that when I came around I was back in the room, my room, tucked into the bed. The television was on, showing some kind of talk show and, sat in the chair with his back to me, was a man. I tried to speak but could not make a sound come out. *It must be the anesthetics,* I thought. I tried to move my arms but had no luck with that, either. This was the first time that I had had surgery, during my adult life, at least. I was unsure of what was normal and what was not so I waited, certain that I would regain some sensation shortly. It felt like an age before the man turned towards me, and if I had been physically able to, I may well have recoiled from the sight of his face.

He instantly reminded me of a comic book villain, severe burns causing the left-hand side of his face and neck to appear discoloured and lumpy. His left eye was no longer present and, rather than opting to wear any form of eye-patch, his face featured a gaping black hole instead.

"How is the patient feeling?" he asked, in a voice much more well-spoken and confident than I had expected. I could not answer, my mouth barely moving. "Ah, yes. You won't be able to speak yet; I'm afraid. Can you blink?" I tried blinking and found this to be manageable. "One for yes, two for no. Are you feeling alright?" *Of course not! I can't move or talk!* I blinked twice. "I see," he said, seemingly unsurprised. "Well, I'm Doctor Yambus," he told me. "I performed your operation. That was quite a lump you had there! However, I'm afraid I have a bit of bad news." My eyes felt wide, worried about what was coming next. "It turned out that the lump, which we had hoped was simply a ganglion cyst, was actually an egg. Rather unusual, I would say. Nevertheless, don't worry, we dealt with it, and all those little buggers which came spewing out as soon as the scalpel hit it!"

The doctor said this with a chuckle, as if what he was telling me was an amusing anecdote that he was sharing at a cocktail party. My mind raced, wanting to know more about what had happened yet unable to speak. I attempted to concentrate my mind onto the foot, to try to detect anything out of the ordinary but there was nothing. Terror began to creep in as I realized that I could not feel any parts of my body.

"I bet you'd like to start feeling again," the doctor declared, as if he had read my mind. "Even so, trust me, you won't want to just yet. Would you like to watch the surgery? We record all of our procedures for the medical students; I can put it on for you if you'd like?" I paused, unsure if I really wanted to see my foot being cut open. *If I have no way of looking at my actual foot, then I suppose it's my only choice,* I thought. I blinked once.

"Jolly good," the doctor said, a sly look appearing across his face. "I have some things to attend to, so I'll leave you to it." Once he had pressed some buttons on the televisions remote, the doctor left the room, leaving me to view the gruesome reality of what I had been through. The video began with my unconscious body being wheeled into an operating theatre by the young anesthetist. I appeared as I expected to look, the mask still attached to my face, the hospital gown covering my body, one surgical stocking in place. The first few minutes showed the doctor making preparations as he painted my foot with an orange liquid, drawing a line across the lump with black marker pen which I presumed to indicate the planned incision line. I was surprised that there were no other medical staff present, and as I pondered this, I watched the doctor move towards my foot with the scalpel. *An egg?!* I wondered, trying to convince myself that I had misheard him. However, I had not. I watched with widening eyes as the blade opened up the top of my foot, a jet of thick black liquid squirting from the newly formed entrance. If I had been able to gasp, that would have been the time to do it.

There was no sound on the video, so I could not tell if the doctor had anything to say, but he did keep looking toward the camera. With a length of dressing, he cleaned away the black mess until the opening was more visible, before beginning to scrape out the contents of the growth. It was next that I saw what he meant, the little buggers. One, then another, then a handful more. Small, black bugs of some description came jumping out of the wound, I would guess that they were the size of little flies. No sooner had they landed on the surrounding skin than they seemed to disappear again. It took me a moment to realize that they had not disappeared at all, instead they had immediately burrowed their way back inside me. More and more emerged from the opening, reaching further up my leg before disappearing from sight.

The doctor turned toward the camera once again, but I could not hear what was being said. As he turned back to his patient, a frenzy appeared to take over him as he tried to rid me of the infestation. Scalpel in hand, he stabbed at my legs, digging holes as he tried to coax the creatures out of my body. I watched in horror as he inflicted the wounds, my gown beginning to turn a terrifying shade of red. I lost count of the times that my skin had been pierced. The doctor turned toward the stainless-steel table beside him and picked up a pair of scissors, proceeding to cut my gown down the middle. He pulled both sides away so that they hung from each side of my bed as he eyed my bare chest. It looked as though he was checking for any signs that I had been bored into by whatever had made a home inside my foot and, just when I thought that it was all clear, he launched another ferocious attack, dotting my whole body with shallow wounds.

Finally, as I lie there soaked in blood, a gaping black hole in my foot, the doctor appeared to be satisfied. He took one last look at the camera before choosing the hacksaw from the table. If it was not for my paralysis, I imagine that I would have vomited as I watched him remove my foot, placing it into a clear plastic bag. He disappeared off camera for a moment, carrying my foot with him, and returned with the anesthetist. They spoke to one another briefly, as he pointed out the wounds that he had inflicted on me. I watched her nodding in agreement to whatever she was being told, before walking away. Then the video ended and I lay there, in shock.

I could not move my body. I could not feel anything and worse than this, I could not even see the damage that had been done as I was unable to remove the duvet. The video had only been ended for a minute or two before the doctor returned to the room.

"Are you OK?" he asked, somewhat stupidly. I blinked twice. "I know it's a lot to take in. There's no hurry. Let me explain what has happened." The doctor continued to stand above me, his deformed face staring into my paralyzed one. "As you saw, you had an infestation. It's rare, but it does happen. We've taken a sample from you, as you could see." *That was my foot, not a bloody sample!* I thought, unable to say it aloud. "Unfortunately, these little critters are rather hardy, not all that easy to kill; you see. Which is why we've had to take some precautions, to stop them spreading to the outside world." My mind struggled from this point on as the doctor explained that I had to be given a drug, one I had not heard of, which effectively prevented me from being able to move, or feel. He had to tell me three times before I understood that this was now permanent. "You are a host," he told me, seeming to relish the condition that I had somehow found myself suffering from. "Which is why we need to keep you here."

Briefly, Dr Yambus disappeared from sight, returning from the bathroom with a mirror that he had removed from the wall. He looked at my eyes with his one eye as he held the mirror above me. It was angled as such that I could see my chest.

"You see?" he asked. I looked at the reflection, taking in the numerous wounds, now coated in dried blood. However, this was not the worst of it for they would heal. Spread across my chest were four lumps, much smaller than the one that had been on my foot, but clearly there and undoubtedly growing. If one had been enough to amputate my foot, I knew then that I could not survive this.

"Get some rest," the doctor told me, grinning as though he took pleasure in my predicament. "We may need to operate shortly."

THE DEVIL'S POCKET WATCH

Tess had always kept it secure, ever since her grandmother had entrusted her with it. *It was a great responsibility,* she had been told. As with anything that seemed to be lacking in evidence, Tess had been doubtful about its power, but she would not need to wait long to get the proof that she needed. She had never known her grandmother to lie; not about anything. She had also always appeared right minded and rational, not being drawn into the religious observations that had control over the rest of their family. Tess's mother, on the other hand, was not sane. She was also, by the time that Tess had turned fourteen, not alive either. It was not as if Tess had suffered some horrific childhood, raised solely by a mother now rarely spoken of it had just been a very conservative upbringing. This boiled down to virtually any pleasurable activity being viewed as a sin and, therefore, strictly prohibited.

For the first fourteen years of Tess's life, her grandmother was there as a person of comfort to her. Their bond strengthened considerably as Tess entered her teenage years, the changes to her body and mind becoming difficult for her mother to cope with. *It's as if she was never a teenage girl,* Tess thought on many occasions. Having at no time been allowed to date, or to stay out as late as her limited number of friends were, or to utter the intermittent profanity if she was to stub a toe, Tess yearned for rebellion. She had vented to her friends at school almost every day, jealous of how much more reasonable their parents appeared to be. She was coming to an age where spending time with her peers was much more important to her than spending time with her mother; she was finding her place in the world.

Tess's mother was repetitive in her warnings, trying to assure her daughter that the rules were in place for a good reason; *safety*. This was always the reason that was given and, perhaps if this was the only reason, then Tess could have accepted things in a more understanding way. Safety was not the main reason for her mother's rules and whenever a disagreement ensued, it was made perfectly clear that if Tess did not follow her mother's directions, then her soul would be spending eternity in a fiery pit.

"I'd take that over living with you!" Tess retorted on one occasion, and only one. Convinced that the Devil himself was speaking through Tess, her mother dealt with the statement in, what she called, a controlled manner. Tess's knuckles had turned purple from the wooden spoon that her mother had taken to her on that day, and she learned not to talk back from that point on. She also learned that her mother was a hypocrite; spouting on about 'loving thy neighbour' yet willing to attack her own child.

Three months after the assault, (this is what Tess, dramatically, called the incident), her mother was dead. It was ruled a suicide, ingestion of some kind of toxin. Despite this conclusion being reached, there were no traces found on the toxicology report. Tess did not see the body; her grandmother would not allow it, and this was certainly for the best. Tess was aware that her mother had been found lying across the bed, as stiff as a board. Her throat had been swollen up, causing suffocation. Her neck was red and raw with bloody scratch marks, self-inflicted from her clawing at it. Her eyes were wide open when Tess's grandmother had discovered the body, bulging almost out of their sockets. The coroner had decided that the injuries were consistent with a neurotoxin which causes a reaction similar to anaphylactic shock. This suggestion, coupled with the revelation that her mother had been taking anti-psychotic medication for a number of years and no evidence of foul play, led to the ruling of suicide.

"I really don't understand it," Tess had told her grandmother on the day of the funeral. *"She thought that suicide was a mortal sin, unforgivable. I just don't see that she would do it. Even if she wanted to."* Her grandmother said nothing, and although she looked sad, she smiled at Tess and held her close. It was an upsetting day, of course, as most funerals inevitably are. Once it was over, however, things started to get better for Tess and ignoring the crushing feelings of guilt, which crept up on her regularly, she knew that she was happier now that her mother had gone.

Being raised by her grandmother was far more pleasant and as she was essentially a well-behaved child, the two of them got on well. They compromised when Tess wanted to make plans that weren't immediately agreed to. Her grandmother gave her just enough freedom to learn from her mistakes and could see that this approach worked wonders to quell the rebellious nature that had been brewing in her granddaughter. Tess found that she wanted to spend time with her new guardian; enjoying her company and even, sometimes, turning down invitations from friends to stay home and hear her stories.

On the day that Tess turned eighteen, her grandmother woke her with breakfast. On the tray, next to a plate of warm eggs, were two items; a small box and an envelope. Tess opened the envelope first, expecting it to be only a birthday card. Instead, Tess also found a cheque. A much larger cheque than expected one, at that.

"It's not to all go on drinks!" she had been told playfully. Tess moved on to the box and the item inside took her breath away. Among the tissue paper sat a pocket watch, more intricately designed than she could have imagined to be possible.

"It's beautiful!" Tess told her grandmother as she flipped open the cover to reveal the watch's face.

"It's special. I need to talk to you about it," her grandmother replied, her voice taking on a more serious tone. She looked a little frightened. *"The watch was given to me by my mother, and she was given it by her mother. It has been passed from mother to eldest daughter for centuries; I have no idea how many generations now."*

"Why did you not give it to my mother then?" Tess asked, a little confused that the tradition had been broken

"It is no ordinary watch, and your mother would not have been a suitable guardian for it. It requires a, shall we say, sounder mind to ensure that it is kept safe."

"I'm sorry Grandma," Tess began, trying to phrase her question delicately. *"Are you saying it's magical in some way??"* Her grandmother just nodded slowly. *"And yet,"* Tess continued, *"You say my mother was not sane enough to look after it?"*

"I see your point, and magical is possibly not the best word for it. I have a duty to explain it all, and I am more than aware of how crazy it sounds at first. The story goes that the watch once belonged to your very distant relation, Polly Matthews. This is going back many hundreds of years, of course. Polly was burned at the stake, a common practice at the time, for being a witch. Whether or not she was a witch is impossible to say, they would burn people for having an epileptic seizure in those days! The tale has been passed on for generations, that the watch once belonged to the Devil himself, and that it has the power to claim souls for hell."

"Right," Tess stated, sarcastically. "Well it's a good yarn Grandma. And it really is a lovely watch. Tess's grandmother just stared at her, silently. *"You don't actually believe that, do you?"* Tess asked, incredulously. *"I mean, you can't!"*

"I didn't at first, well I suppose I never really did for a long time. I mean, I used the watch each day and, as far as I can tell, it hasn't whisked my soul off to eternal damnation! Nevertheless, something happened; I suppose it pretty much confirmed the story for me. Paradoxically, now that I know what it can do I will never be able to look in its face again."

Tess stared blankly, wondering why her sane and rational grandmother was now talking about demonic watches.

"You're making no sense at all. And you're giving me the creeps a bit too so can I just eat my eggs please. Thank you for the money, what should I spend it on?" Tess asked, trying to change the subject.

"I don't want you to believe me, you shouldn't really. You just need to trust me enough to make sure it's kept safe and that no-one other than you

uses it. Promise me, please," her grandmother pleaded.

"So, let me try to get this straight," Tess said, a little impatiently. *"It's only unsafe if you believe it is, therefore, it's safe for me because I don't. However, despite not believing that it's dangerous, I'm to treat it as though it were? And if that's the case, what happened to make you think this thing has some kind of unexplainable power?"*

"I can't tell you. I'm sorry. If I did, and you accepted what I said as truth, then I would be putting you in danger. Can you just promise me that you'll keep it safe? It's a lovely watch, there is no reason for you not to look after it regardless of the reasons."

"Of course, I'll keep it safe, and obviously I'll pass it on to my daughter if I ever have one. However, I think you might be going a little senile in your old age," Tess teased. *"It really is harmless, see."* As she uttered these words, Tess flipped open the cover to reveal that clock face and pointed it directly at her grandmother. Before she had a chance to look away, the elderly lady began to gasp for breath, her weak, arthritic hands clawing at her throat as it swelled. There was almost no time to act and by the time Tess had thrown her tray of breakfast to one side and jumped out of bed her grandma had taken her last breath.

Tess now believed, for it was too great a coincidence to not be true. The part about the soul being dragged off to hell still seemed far-fetched but there was no doubting that something evil was lurking within the watch. Fearful of meeting the same fate, Tess guarded the watch at all times, too afraid to open it herself. The circumstances surrounding her mother's death weighed heavy upon her mind for many years to come, as Tess deliberated what had actually happened. She would never know for certain, but this may have been for the best. After all, there had been enough trauma in Tess's young life already. Knowing that, propelled by an inclination to improve her grandchild's life, as well as a curiosity about the trinket she had guarded for almost fifty years, Tess's grandmother had deliberately cast her own daughter's soul into the pit and inadvertently sealed the same fate for herself, would have been an unbearable burden. Tess did, however, manage to live a long life with one drawback. She was barren, there was no way around it, and there was to be no-one to pass on the watch to.

It's a sign, she thought, distraught by the state of the world with its wars and destruction. As the end of her life approached, Tess took the watch to an antique's store and placed it among the other items without attracting anyone's attention. The Devil *can take as many souls as he wants now.*

Collection II:
Tunnels & Other Stories

21

A picture-perfect family; Mum, Dad, two boys and a really pretty girl. They had arrived yesterday. I watched them through the trees as they positioned that new-looking caravan into place, under the direction of the campsite owners. It was hot, and I was sweating under my camouflage. But I couldn't very well wear anything else and risk being seen. I returned today. I continued to watch, studying the way they interacted with each other. They all had smiles on their faces; not a care in the world. It was mid-afternoon; it wouldn't be dark for another five or six hours. I could wait. There was no way of knowing how long they would be staying for so it had to happen tonight, I couldn't risk coming back tomorrow only to find they had gone.

The site was perfect in so many ways. It was relaxed, especially from a security aspect. It was accessible on three sides to anyone willing to walk through the dense trees; the only vehicular access came from one long, unlit lane. There was no gated entry, nothing to stop the guests coming and going at any time that they chose. Such a stroke of luck that I found it; this will be much easier than last time. That place had turned into an absolute nightmare, and it could so easily have been my final time.

The build-up, the routine, the planning. These were the parts that held the most excitement for me. The watching. It was like a military operation, and I was good at it. Even if the army didn't want me. That was their loss, their mistake. Maybe if they had taken me in, I wouldn't be doing this now. Perhaps that pretty family would have been able to enjoy their holiday without having it cut short. For an hour I stood among the trees, motionless, just my eyes moving around as I surveyed the other campers.

It was much less busy than the places I had been to previously. One side of the field, to the east of the entry point, it was filled with caravans, all nearly identical. They appeared to be the same size; four-berth most likely. I counted them up yesterday; eleven of them. Still all eleven there. I had walked by last night, a little after midnight, for a kind of reconnaissance mission; I wanted to see if anyone would notice me, but they didn't. They never do. None of the caravans looked as if they were up to traveling, and it was almost certain that they were left there all year round. Which meant there was a good chance that they were empty, or certainly most of them.

In the south-eastern corner, there were three tents, large ones. Could have been ten or twelve-man tents, all arranged with the entrances facing each other, surrounding a square of windbreakers. Within the windbreakers were chairs, cooking equipment, and so on. The residents, whom I assumed were one large group, had been the only ones still up when I took my wander last night. Seven adults, sitting around a fire drinking beer and cursing whilst their hoard of unruly offspring tried to get to sleep. Thankfully no dogs this time. I hate dogs.

The new family were as far from everyone as they could be, claiming a solo pitch on the western edge of the field. They must think they are too good to set up close to the others; and maybe they are right. Even so, that arrogance only serves to make my life so much easier. I struggled to pull myself away, absorbed in the game that the children were playing. I watched in amusement as the older boy and girl threw a ball to each other, to the annoyance of their younger brother who stood no chance in catching it. Eventually, he stopped trying, stomping away and calling for his mummy. I watched as the older boy, a tall, dark-haired creature with a wicked grin, shouted after his brother; "Stop being such a baby, you little loser!" The kid must have been four or five and, briefly, I felt a little pity for him. I stared at the older boy. *You'll be first*, I promised him. Only a few more hours to go; time to finish the preparations.

I returned a little after dusk, following the lane but staying just within the tree line in case any cars drove by. No-one came along the dark road; all remained silent until I reached the entrance to the site. This was the riskiest part; the twenty or thirty yards that ran alongside the toilets and showers were well lit and stayed that way all night. The coast looked clear, but there was no way of knowing if someone was about to come out of the toilets. I just needed to walk confidently, as if I belonged there. I felt my heart beat more quickly, the adrenalin flooding my system. I heard a toilet flush as I took a few hurried steps into the darkness, just beyond the reach of the lights. Seconds later, I was standing against the western edge, completely enveloped in darkness, as I watch an overweight female in a dressing gown make her way back towards the trio of tents in the far corner.

I looked towards my destination and saw four people sat around a fire; their faces illuminated by the flames. The youngest was missing, presumably already asleep inside the caravan. My right hand reached into the deep pocket of my cargo pants, caressing the switchblade that waited there. *Only for emergencies,* I reminded myself. I took sideways steps, hidden by the blackness, as I edged closer to them. The caravan was positioned almost up to the edge, with perhaps three or four feet between the rear of it and the start of the woodland. I took a step back, slipping into the pitch blackness, avoiding the light which shone from the caravan's window.

My plan hinged largely on one hope; that it would be a warm enough evening for them to leave a window open. If not, then I would need to force the door which, although not impossible, would increase the risks considerably. I was in luck, however, as I saw three of the windows still wide open. In the past, I had managed to get inside before the owners, hiding myself in the built-in closet of a larger caravan. When this one arrived, I considered repeating that plan as it had worked out well before. I searched on-line for the floor plan, located a suitable hiding place, and kept my fingers crossed. It would work, I knew that, but they were sat too near the door for me to be able to sneak in. Plan B was the windows, which relied on them not to close them before heading to bed. *It's a warm and sticky evening,* I thought. *It'll be fine, just wait it out.* Half an hour later, I watched as mum ushered the two siblings inside, the mean boy and the pretty girl, drawing the curtains. After another ten minutes of watching dad prodding at the fire with a stick, mum returned.

She made her way to her partner; a duvet wrapped around her despite the warmth of the evening. I watched from my position, alone in the dark, as she sat on his lap. I could make out a slight rhythm to their motion as they kissed, and I wondered if they were doing more beneath that duvet. I only watched, transfixed, certain that they must want to be seen if they are behaving like that in the open. I felt a brief wave of confusion as I looked upon them with both disgust and arousal, but their moment came to a sudden end with the call of a child. From the muffled sounds, I made out that the smallest child was awake, mum to the rescue as she headed inside. Dad, a tall, thin man in his early forties, gathered up the empty cans and tidied up a little before following her inside. It was almost time and the nerves began to set in, the twisting, knotted butterflies felt that they wanted to burst from my stomach.

Remaining still for fear of crunching a branch beneath my feet, I stood transfixed on the caravan, willing off the lights. There was no way to see in with the curtains closed. I checked my watch; almost eleven. The lights went out at eleven-twenty. The windows were left open. I took a step forward and paused. My eagerness may have almost led to disaster. *If they were doing what it looked like, and haven't finished, then they are probably carrying on now,* I pondered. *Give them a bit longer. Be patient.* I crept alongside the caravan, trying to listen for any sounds that would indicate anyone was awake. There was nothing; no television, no talking, no sex noises.

I took one last glance across the field; only the large group in the far corner showed any signs of life, but they would not be able to see me from there. I peered around the front to check the coupling and found the caravan to still be attached to the Range Rover. I slipped by backpack off and unzipped it, straightening out the tubing and feeding one end through the open window. There were so many things that could go wrong, and I did not like not knowing exactly where each of them was sleeping. Nevertheless, it had to be done. I fixed my end of the tube to the unit I had designed myself and switched it on. The battery whirred, seeming much louder in the silence of the field than it had previously. I positioned it beneath the caravan and scurried back under the cover of darkness among the trees. I waited. Ten minutes. Then another ten. There was no change, no sounds, no lights coming on. *Now or never!* I made my way to collect the equipment, placing it safely back inside my bag. The contents of the vapour were my own variation on a recipe in the Chemical Warfare Handbook, utilizing the effects of a veterinary tranquilizer that should have rendered the caravan's occupants unconscious by now. If the dose had been evenly taken in, I'd expect the larger people to come around in two to three hours. But that little boy would be a different matter; it could be eight hours. And that's if he even wakes up at all.

I attached my small, homemade gas mask to my face and managed to pop the catch on the door with the switchblade, closing it quietly behind me. They looked so peaceful; the three children on a pile of duvets across the main living space. I crept past them, opening the first of two doors on my right. A toilet. I carefully opened the second door and found the parents in bed, a duvet covering them up to their heads, appearing as if asleep. Satisfied that all was going to plan, I clicked on my torch and began to search for the keys. Not anywhere obvious in the living space. *Must be in his jeans. Bingo.* I found them lying among the clothes he had dumped on the floor before climbing into bed, slipped them into my pocket, and made my way outside. I locked the caravan, despite being almost certain that its occupants would not awaken during the journey. *Just in case,* I told myself. *Don't want anyone jumping out and making a scene.*

Sliding into the driver's seat, I turned the key, allowing the Rover's engine to purr. I couldn't see anyone else on the campsite but decided that there was enough open space for me to move around towards the entrance before switching on the lights. Once I had the car facing the lit-up area around the facilities, I flicked on the headlights, and we were on our way. I had at least two hours until anyone began to stir and, to be on the safe side, I had selected a destination only an hour away. I was confident that it was far enough from the original extraction point and would also afford me ample time to get my guests into position. The campsite would not necessarily raise any concerns over guests leaving earlier than planned; after all, they had paid upfront on arrival so no loss to the owners. Chances are there would be a few days before anyone reported them missing and by then, I would be long gone.

Fifty-minutes later, I turned the Range Rover on to a chalky, quarry path. The location was isolated; dark and silent. The structures surrounding the path were parts of a disused steel works; great, red clunks of metal protruding from the ground, rising all around me. I dragged the caravan along until I was out of sight of the road, parking it up next to the steel barn which had acted as a makeshift staff room long ago. Yanking open the door with a clang of metal, the sound echoing around me, I went inside to grab supplies. One bag of cable ties and a dirty sheet, which I cut into five long strips. We were far enough from anyone that screams for help would go unanswered, but I did not want to have to listen to five people yelling at me. It made me anxious, and when I get anxious I can become disorganized and confused. But there was no confusion as to why I was there at that moment for I knew, beyond any doubt, that it was the only way that I could be taken seriously. The only way that those bastards who dismissed me as a freak, as not good enough, as an idiot - that they would know my name.

Cautiously, I unlocked the caravan and opened the door, slowly. Still no sign of movement. I began with the adults as they posed the most threat to me, removing the duvet and binding their hands and feet with cable ties, wrapping the dirty cloth around their mouths. Still they did not stir. I looked down at them on the bed, both fully nude, bound and helpless. My thoughts sank into the gutter for a moment as I looked at her; she would never know. *No!* I told myself. *That's not who you are. That's not what you want to be remembered as.* I repeated the process with the three children, all of whom were clothed in pyjamas, and stood outside to wait. Thirty-six minutes passed before I heard a thud.

Re-entering the caravan, I saw the three children still out for the count. It was the adults that had come around first, just as I had expected; their larger masses would have recovered from the toxin more quickly than their children could. I cocked my head to the side as I gazed down at him, naked and restrained, trying pathetically to drag himself along the floor. He couldn't lift his head high enough to see me properly, so he rolled himself over, the gag muffling whatever obscenities he was attempting to throw in my direction. I allowed myself a little laugh.

"If only you could see how ridiculous you look!" I told him, enjoying my position of power. "Helpless on the floor, flapping that tiny thing about." I glanced at his manhood. "Are you cold?" He writhed about on the floor in anger, his eyes wide as he assessed his situation. "Is that pretty lady awake yet?" I asked. This seemed to refuel his anger, his protectiveness becoming even more evident. "Oh, don't worry. It's not like that. I'm not that kind of monster." I stepped over him to check the bedroom and found her in the fetal position, sobbing as best she could with the rag in her mouth.

"Don't worry, honey," I told her. "It'll be over soon enough. I need you two to come with me; I know it'll be difficult to walk in your situation, but I'll help you up and you'll need to try. OK?" She just continued to sob, making no attempt to get off of the bed or even look at me. *Rude,* I thought, approaching the man.

"Looks like you're up first then," I told him, putting my hand under his armpits and dragging him towards the door. He wouldn't stay still, which I guess is understandable, but it made the process difficult for me. I don't cope with stress very well; it makes me itchy. Once I had his head poking out of the door, facing down at the three small steps, I moved behind him for the last push. He landed in a heap in the dust, groaning loudly as his shoulder made a popping sound. "Dislocated, most likely," I told him. Still he kept trying to talk to me, perhaps to beg and plead, perhaps to threaten me. Whatever message he wanted to convey was in vain, I had made the mistake of talking to them before, and it only muddled me up. *They're the enemy, they will say anything to stop you carrying on with your work, they would kill you if they could,* I reminded myself. I locked the caravan and dragged him into the barn, under the glow of electric lights that I had fixed up on the previous day. He scouted around the room, clocking the chairs. Five chairs.

It was difficult, but I hauled him onto one of the chairs, wrapping ten feet of thick, electrical cable around him for extra security. Now, even if he tried to stand, he would be taking the chair with him. "I need you to stay here," I told him, leaning forward a little so out eyes could meet. "Do you understand?" He nodded, panic across his face. "If you move, I'll kill someone." Again, he nodded.

The children still did not stir, so I picked up the smallest. He was light enough for me to carry out without any problem. Only he didn't feel right; paler than I expected. *Shit!* The gas *was* too much for his mass; I suspected it may be. *He's going to go berserk when he finds out!* I told myself, knowing that I needed to get everyone restrained in the barn at the same time. I decided to put the little child on the chair furthest from his father, in the hope that he would think he was still only unconscious. I strapped him in under his father's glare, but this time he did not try to speak to me.

The other two kids weren't an issue; both light enough to carry, both only beginning to stir. Four out of five in place. Ten minutes, maximum, I had spent between grabbing the last child and returning to the caravan. In the space of those ten minutes, she had gone from helplessly restrained on the bed to having disappeared. There weren't any hiding places inside, she was not in the toilet, and she surely could not have walked far. I glanced around in a panic - the utensil drawer was open. *Could she have dragged herself to the drawer and found something to cut the ties with? It wouldn't be easy but not impossible. Shit! Stupid me for thinking she was being complicit, just lying there.*

"I have your whole family in here," I yelled from the barn door. "I suggest you get here now, or I'm going to start taking bits off of them." Nothing. I scanned around with my torch, but she could be anywhere. *Fuck!*

"Right," I told the man. "I'm going to take your gag off. I want you to call her back here, right now! If she doesn't come back quickly, then I kill him." I pointed my switchblade at the body of the youngest child. His father's eyes widened, nodding quickly.

"Helen!" he yelled. "You have to come back. Please. He's going to kill Harry!" As he shouted these words, I heard muffled screams coming from behind me, the older children having woken up into this nightmare. I flashed my torch out of the barn door, revealing nothing of Helen's whereabouts.

"I warned you!" I hissed, before standing behind little Harry and jabbing my blade through his neck. A steady stream of red sprayed from his jugular as tears fell from my prisoners. They did not need to know he was already dead; not that it would have made their loss any more bearable. I stepped behind that taller boy, the one who had been horrible to Harry earlier that day. Looking to his father, I repeated my threat. "Get her back here. Now!" Helen's disappearance spoiled things for me; I felt rushed in case she managed to get help. This is not how it was meant to be and, if I couldn't find her, then I would be one person short of target. Someone else's blood would be on her hands.

Four times he called to Helen, all to no avail. I stood, once again, at the entrance to the barn with a torch in one-hand and a blood-stained blade in the other.

"Helen!" I called. "I'm counting to ten. Then your lanky shit of a son is dead." I paused, listening intently into the darkness. Still nothing. "Then I'll count to ten again, before slitting your daughter's throat. You'd better hurry up."

"Please don't," the man begged.

"It's hardly my fault!" I told him. "You married a right selfish bitch! She could have done what she was told, and little Harry would still be alive. Admittedly, not for very long, but she did cut his life a bit short." He did not know how to reply to me, staring instead, anger flickering in his eyes. I shouted towards the door. "Ten, nine.." I counted down, slowing a little as I approached the final number. Still nothing. *She's gone. Somehow.* It wasn't how I'd planned it, but the end result would be the same. Doing my best to appear in control, I walked up to that gangly youth and ended him with five rapid jabs of the switchblade to his chest. His eyes widened for a brief moment as blood gurgled from his mouth, and then nothing. Another life extinguished in a moment.

I turned to see his father attempt to run at me, ankles bound, a chair on his back, but he did not get far. I resisted using the knife on him, merely shoving him backwards with a crash of wood and a yelp from his already damaged shoulder. His daughter cried incessantly, but the gag stifled the sound enough for it not to bother me too much. I looked at her, staring a while until she turned her gaze from the floor to meet mine. She knew she would be next as well as I did, but the look of fear had changed to a look of acceptance, of sadness about something that she could not change. I felt something when our eyes met, something that I was not used to. *Remorse? Guilt?* I knew I was a monster; I never denied that. But I had an agenda, a target to reach. And it was not as if I did not value human life, or even that I enjoyed the killing. It was the hunt that I enjoyed, that I was good at. But I could not very well go to all the effort of extracting people and then letting them go afterward? I'd have been caught years ago if I did that!

Helen's apparent escape had presented a problem for me, and this was something I had not prepared for. It had never happened before, but perhaps I had become greedy. Or just wanted it to be over. The highest number of kills, confirmed kills that is, by any British serial killer is twenty. Some lady from long ago with a penchant for poison. Of course, that crazy doctor confessed to killing over two hundred a few years back, but it hasn't been proved. So, I want twenty-one. That would make *me* the most prolific serial killer this country has ever seen. As I gazed at the girl, trying to identify what I was feeling at that moment, I thought back to the girl a few months ago; number 16. It was planned down to the last detail; her morning jogging route, the most secluded spots along it, the ideal method. I saw it as an assassination, a necessary target. I could not put my finger on it, but there was something about her that made her stand out. It could have been an air of superiority, a woman well beyond my reach, an annoyance she evoked simply by jogging past me that first time. The hit had been easy. I'd lunged at her as she passed some beach huts along a promenade, pulling her between two of them and slitting her throat. Then I was gone. Number 16. I just needed five more, and I could relax; it wouldn't matter if I got away with it for any longer. If Helen doesn't return, then I'm still one short and that won't do.

"One, two..." I began, loudly towards the door. "Nine, ten." Nothing. ""She really doesn't care about you lot, does she!" I declared, incredulous that a mother could run from her family in this way. "Well, she can't have gotten far," I stated, with a sigh. "You know I can't let you go," I told him, as he continued to grunt from his place on the floor. "But it would be monstrous of me to make you watch another of your children die. I'll give you this small mercy." I leaned down towards him, the reddened blade pointing at his neck. He fell silent, just staring into me in defiance. His gaze was fixed, even in death. The loss of life happened too quickly for his eyes to close, as my blade entered the side of his head, piercing through his left ear. The entire five inches went in, destroying his brain in a fraction of a second, gloopy grey and red lumps sticking to the knife as I retrieved it. He slumped to the floor, a dark pool forming around the wound. His daughter now having fallen silent; she knew what was coming.

I sat on the floor, talking to the girl for some time after killing her father. Not about anything especially meaningful, and the conversation was entirely one-sided, but it passed some time while I deliberated my options. What I needed to do was kill the girl and then find Helen. But in keeping the child alive for a while longer, perhaps it would draw Helen back once she realized that she could not get far. Only she *had* got far, much farther than I had expected anyway. If she had waited to return with the police, then my time would have been up; of that I have no doubt. And I would have been named Britain's second most prolific serial killer, meaning that nineteen people had died for nothing. However, she did not return with the police. My one-sided conversation was cut short by the sound of tyres on gravel outside the barn; the space illuminated by headlights. I jumped from my seated position and waited to the side of the open door, knife at the ready, listening as car doors opened and closed.

"Jesus Christ!" I heard an older-sounding man exclaim. "We should have waited for the police!"

"I couldn't," came Helen's distraught voice. I saw the outline of her figure take a step inside the barn, surveying the blood-soaked bodies of her husband and two of her children. She looked as though she would collapse, but she spotted her daughter still alive, and ran to try to free her. The police were on their way, and I knew there was little time. I stayed motionless for a moment, and this must have given the Good Samaritan the idea that the coast was clear. He edged his way into the barn, and I struck; quick, repeated jabs with the blade until he dropped to the floor. Helen frantically pulled at the cable ties that bound her daughter, but she could not free her. So, I did.

"I only need one more," I told them. I looked at the girl and told her to run. To this day, I'm not sure why I had the sudden change of heart; maybe I wanted to leave a witness to describe the cold-blooded nature of my actions, maybe I grew a morsel of conscience. She looked to her mother, as if needing permission. Helen nodded sadly, and the girl was gone. I stared into Helen's eyes as I raised my blade, her face suddenly illuminated in the reflection of blue and red lights now coming from outside. My time was almost up, but I reached my goal with a swift slash of the throat; the warm, sticky spray coating my face before I dropped to my knees and placed my hands on my head. My work was complete, and now came the prize - the fame, the respect, and the notoriety.

The Box

Almost twenty years after he had finally been brave enough to start up his own business, Jack was finally bringing in enough money for his wife, Lisa, to not have to work. The majority came from carrying out house clearances, but he was also earning a noticeable amount on the side, selling on the items that he cleared which he deemed too good for the tip. Largely selling online, and studying countless antique and collectible guidebooks, he made a tidy profit selling everything from ornaments to toys, vintage clothing to antique furniture. The guidebooks were a huge help, pointing him in the right direction as to whether the items were worth selling at all and if so, how much he could hope to get for them. In his collection, it was almost guaranteed that anything of value would be listed there somewhere, which is why Jack was so puzzled that he could not find anything resembling the item in his hand.

"What do you think this is?" he asked Lisa, as he made his way to the kitchen. She said nothing, only turning to look at what he held in his hand. As he passed it to her, she studied the intricate patterns carved into all six faces of the cube, running her fingers across the smoothness of the black marble. Each side looked to be around six inches, the pattern only being disturbed by a groove running all the way around, an inch below, presumably, the top. On one face, there appeared to be a tiny keyhole, indicating that the box could be opened.

"Do you have the key?" Lisa asked, gently shaking the box. "It doesn't sound like there's anything in it."

"No key that I could see. There weren't any boxes of junk, just large items really. And I can't find this in any of the books, but it's too nice to throw out."

"God, don't throw it away! It's really pretty," Lisa said, still transfixed by the patterns which had been so meticulously etched into the marble.

"As long as you're sure?" Jack asked. "You said I'm not allowed to keep any more junk in the house!"

"There's something different about this, we should keep it if you don't think it's worth much."

"Well, if it is, then it isn't listed in any of the books. But I'll have a look online later and see if I can find anything similar." With all searches failing to provide any information, the box found itself placed on the mantelpiece alongside a host of other ornamental items which Lisa had given him permission to hold on to. And there it remained, for almost a fortnight.

When Jack had begun his business, his oldest child, Steven, was eight. He was now twenty-seven, with a child of his own; four-year-old Maisie. Jack's granddaughter was a whirlwind; at least, that was how they all affectionately referred to her. One Sunday each month the Jack and Lisa would cook a meal for their son, his wife, and Maisie, and every time something would get broken by the four-year-old bull in a china shop. It was never malicious; she was just clumsy, and her parents would apologize profusely each time. Usually, it was picture frames getting knocked from the wall, or glasses knocked from the table during dinner. On this occasion, Maisie's parents made an error of judgment, allowing her to bring a plastic toy with her; one that launched discs at a potentially lethal velocity.

It was as the four adults were chatting in the kitchen, watching pans bubbling away on the hob, that they heard the little shriek. It was a familiar sound, the same noise that Maisie had emitted whenever she had broken something that did not belong to her. As everyone turned to look in the direction of the sound, Steven let out a sigh.

"You may have to start child proofing the house!" he declared. Lisa did not take the comment as a joke.

"Maybe you shouldn't have allowed her to bring a weapon with her!" she stated. "I really think that you need to get her seen; it isn't normal to be breaking stuff all the time."

"She's just being a child," Jack said. "I'm sure it's fine." Steven made his way towards the living room and stopped in his tracks. His daughter was kneeling on the wooden floor, with her back to him, making a heaving sound, as though she were choking on a hair ball.

"Maisie?" he asked. Slowly, she turned towards her father; her hands scrunched tightly into fists. As his gaze moved from her hands to her face, Steven's eyes widened as he saw that the skin around her face was covered in some kind of black powder. The heaving sound stopped as she looked at him, smiling widely, her teeth blackened by whatever substance was on her face.

"Dad!" Steven called, the hint of panic being apparent. Jack made his way into the living room.

"What's happened?" he asked, staring at Maisie. "Shit, she's bleeding," Jack pointed out, noticing the deep red trickles emanating from his closed fists. Steven approached his daughter, taking her hands.

"Open your hands, honey," he said, as calmly as he could manage. By this point, the two women were stood in the doorway, trying to assess the situation before making any suggestions. Maisie continued to grin at her father, looking him in the eye, as she unclenched her fists. As her fingers unfurled, she displayed the fragments of marble, having changed from white to red with the blood. "What is that?" Steven asked, turning to his father.

"Some marble box I found at work. Don't know what it is; it was pretty, so we kept it on the mantelpiece. Honey," Jack said, turning to his granddaughter. "Did you knock it off with your toy?" Maisie did not speak, simply continuing to grin at her father. "You should have just told us. You didn't need to pick it up; come to the bathroom and we'll have a look at your hands." The words seemed to register with the child, despite her silence, and she stood up, hands outstretched, palms upwards.

Lisa led her granddaughter to the bathroom, sending Maisie's mother to fetch the first aid box from a cupboard in the kitchen, while the men cleared up the remaining fragments of the marble box. Positioning the child on the lid of the toilet, Lisa examined her hands. There appeared to be a lot of blood, but once she had used tweezers to remove any fragments that were visible, and wiped over cuts, they did not appear anywhere near as bad, and it was a relief to see that medical treatment would not be required. Following the application of a few plasters, Lisa went on to use a wet wipe to clean Maisie's face. The black substance did not come off easily, leaving streaks of powder, and took some time to remove. Inside of the child's mouth was the most difficult as no-one wanted her to ingest it, so Lisa cleaned as well as she could manage with a damp flannel and ordered Maisie to brush her teeth. By the time the clean-up was deemed to be good enough, their dinner was ready. Through all of this, Maisie had still not uttered a word.

"I think we should get her to a doctor," Steven said, as the group took their places around the table. "We've got no idea what that black stuff was."

"It's Sunday," his wife reminded him. "It'll mean a trip to the hospital."

"I know, but she's not spoken since it happened. Something isn't right." The adults looked towards Maisie, still grinning at her father, not even seeming to have noticed the meal placed before her. "Eat up, before it gets cold," he told her, and they began to work through the roast lamb in silence, each of them glancing at the child who continued to stare, unmoving. By the time that the adults had finished their meals, Maisie had not taken a bite.

"You have to eat something," Lisa told her, stabbing a fork into a piece of meat. "Would you like some help?" Maisie's gaze was unflinching, still focused on her father, but she opened her mouth as if to accept being fed by her grandmother. Lisa took the cue and guided the food into Maisie's mouth, placing the fork back beside the plate. The child began to chew slowly and, suddenly, spat the meat from her mouth.

"Maisie!" her mother gasped.

"It's burnt, mother!" Maisie shouted.

"It most certainly is not," Lisa exclaimed, surprised by the girl's sudden rudeness. "It's a little on the rare side, if anything." Maisie's gaze switched quickly to her grandmother and before anyone could realize what was happening, Lisa felt the jab of the fork in her arm. She looked down and let out a little scream at the sight of all three prongs embedded in her skin. As she looked at Maisie's face, the girl grinned, twisting the fork ninety degrees, opening up the wound. Lisa jumped up from the table, backing away from the child, her good hand clutching her bleeding arm. As soon as the other adults had registered the violent act, they stood quickly, rushing to Lisa's aid. All except Steven, who grabbed his daughter and carried her upstairs.

"What have you done?" he begged, tears forming in his eyes.

"Stupid bitch shouldn't have burned the lamb," Maisie said in a matter-of-fact tone. "Don't be angry Daddy." Steven just stared at his daughter in disbelief.

"I'm sorry Maisie, but I am angry. You have been really naughty. You need to go and see if grandma is OK and apologize."

"Who is Maisie?" the girl enquired, as genuinely as if she was asking any other question to which she expected an answer.

"Don't be silly, I'm not in the mood. You're Maisie."

"I'm Dot." With that, Steven stood up to check on his mother whom he could hear crying from the kitchen. "Don't go, I don't want you to leave me."

"I'm not leaving you; I'm only going to the kitchen. You stay here, please."

"Can I have a kiss before you go?" Maisie asked, sweetly. Steven bent down to kiss his daughter on the cheek, but she turned her head, catching him off-guard, and spitting into his face.

As he entered the kitchen, Jack was dressing Lisa's wound and neither of Steven's parents saw him approach. They only turned as they heard their daughter-in-law let out a gasp.

"What's that over your face?" she asked, staring at her husbands blackened grin. He did not reply. "Steven!" she stated.

"Who is Steven?" he asked, cocking his head to one side. "I'm William." His wife's face displayed a look of panic, of not understanding what was going on. "Would you like some gravy?" Steven asked his wife. She did not answer, not following the question, so he decided for her. Grabbing the porcelain gravy boat from the table, Steven swung it into the side of his wife's head, knocking her to the floor, ceramic shard landing around her. Jack lunged towards his son, reacting to the situation with little thought. As he shoved Steven backwards, Jack felt a sharp burn in his side as he slumped onto the kitchen floor. His eyes were wide with terror as he gazed up at his four-year-old granddaughter, a bloodied carving knife her hands.

"Maisie," he whispered, trembling in shock.

"I'm Dot." Lisa did not stand a chance, fear having frozen her to the spot. She stood at the end of the kitchen, screaming at full volume, as she surveyed the carnage in front of her. She watched as her son knelt down, snapping the neck of his own wife, and felt as though she may pass out. Lisa did not have the opportunity to pass out, or any way of escaping the pain that followed. Her reactions were too slow to hold back the onslaught from the child, whose wild stabs sent Lisa to the floor, soaking the tiles in a deep crimson.

"We should go home now, Dot," Steven told his daughter, and the pair took each other's hands before making their way out onto the street.

"It all looks so different," Maisie said. "Do you know which way to go?"

"We'll find our way home," Steven assured her, and they began to wander in the direction that felt right, the route which would take them back to their recently cleared home, the one they had both died in, the one that had stored their ashes together in a beautiful marble urn.

Retribution

On the night that it happened, revenge was the only thing on my mind. Well, that and anger, shock, despair, and grief. But revenge dominated my thoughts. We were only married a year; not quite a whole year, in fact. It was six days before our first wedding anniversary that I found the front door ajar, a gap of no more than an inch, but enough to stand out as unusual. I was late home and, as much as I was in no way directly responsible for her death, the guilt weighed heavily upon me from that day on. I could have gone straight home from work like I always did. I could have told those people that I worked with, the people I don't even really like, that I would pass on going for a drink. It's my birthday! Melissa said, as excited as a child. Everyone is coming.

It wasn't true; not everyone was there. In our small office, there were twelve employees that day; seven of us walked into the pub. I wish it was six. I was driving, so used that as my excuse to leave after two pints. It was more than I should have had, and was out of character for me but, even at the age of thirty-one, peer pressure still got to me. I told Liz what I was doing. We always knew where the other one was, although I said it was someone from the offices' birthday, rather than naming Melissa. They had never met, and I had no sinister intentions, but I said it anyway.

As I pushed open the door, I called out her name. No reply. My heartbeat increased involuntarily; I don't remember panicking at that point, simply unsure of the situation. My body knew that something was off. I poked my head into each of the downstairs rooms, finding no sign of Liz, no sign of a struggle. I dropped my briefcase in the hallway outside the living room. Still wearing my brogues, I ran up the newly carpeted stairs, making almost no sound. This fact struck me only later; she would not have heard him coming.

The door to our bedroom was closed, and my hands felt clammy as I turned the bronze knob. The door creaked as it opened, something that used to irritate me every night. This time it only added to the dread that was building up inside me. Then I saw her. I took a step forward, my eyes wide, my jaw slack. The crisp white bedding now soaked red, the side of her torso gaping open. I stared in silence, my brain trying to process the image before me. My beautiful wife, face down, fully nude. Dead. I did not dare to touch her, or anything else in the room, until the police arrived. I had seen enough crime series' to know that I would be the prime suspect.

The rest of that evening is a blur. The house was illuminated by flashing red and blue lights from outside; I was sat in the kitchen answering questions. I don't remember the police asking if they should contact anyone, but they must have. I remember my best friend Darren rushing into the house and hugging me. I don't know how long the police were there, but it must have been a few hours by the time the coroner had removed Liz from my life. It was only when they had all left, just Darren and I in the house, that I finally managed to cry. At that point, I did not know any details of Liz's last moments, but her nudity suggested the obvious.

Darren cleaned the room up for me, that much I remember. I couldn't face it and he just marched in there with some bin bags and stripped the bed, wiped down the sides which were still coated in dust from the forensics' guys, and tried his best to make it presentable. The mattress will have to go, he told me, offering to deal with that himself. He was trying to be practical, I suppose. I didn't hear from the police for almost a week, and I had been too timid to chase them up myself. If there was news, they would call, I thought. Then they did call.

They had arrested Steven Hayes. He was a junkie, with a string of previous convictions for burglary and assault. The police took me to a room at the station to talk, showing a mugshot of the man they had arrested. Seeing his face made it worse, only serving to enhance the images I had of him raping my wife. I asked if they were sure he was the one; I wanted to know what evidence they had found. One of your neighbours spotted someone matching his description acting suspiciously near your house that night, I was told. He had a knife on him, which matched the lacerations to your wife's body. He has a string of priors. He has no alibi. It all sounded pretty circumstantial to me, but the detective in command seemed convinced they had the right guy. It would go to trial that week. They would push for the death penalty, giving me the opportunity to apply for 'retribution'.

Capital punishment was only brought back in three years ago, largely to ease the financial burden of having to keep these monsters locked up for such long periods of time. It went to a public vote, narrowly passing. I voted against it; the death penalty always seemed barbaric to me. Now I wasn't so sure. Steven Hayes went to trial and, largely due to his history of serious offences, was found guilty by all twelve members of the jury. The hearing lasted less than a day, and I sat, stone-faced, listening to the prosecution detail how the accused had held Liz down and cut her open. Her time of death had been only one to two hours before I had called it in; I had been laughing in the pub while my wife bled to death. The jurors tutted and shook their heads when they heard that, although no semen had been found, the victim showed signs of having been penetrated with something. There was bruising around her thighs, and she had torn inside. There was no way to tell if this happened before, or after she was killed. The judge handed down the death penalty; the accused said nothing during the entire hearing except to plead 'not guilty'.

"What now?" Darren whispered to me as I watched them escort Hayes out of the court room. I looked at him blankly. "Let them do it or apply for retribution?" I would be lying if I said I hadn't thought about it, after all, revenge is a primal instinct, and I certainly wanted him to suffer. But doing it myself? I couldn't picture it in reality.

"I don't know if I can," I said, feeling guilty for what I saw as my weakness.

"Only you can make that choice, mate," Darren replied. "If it was me, I'd want to do the deed myself. You know they'll only give him the needle, and he'll drift off to sleep. No pain, no suffering. Just think about what Liz went through."

"You think I haven't been? I think about it every fucking day!" I hissed. "I just don't know if killing him myself will make me feel better."

"It will," Darren told me, looking me dead in the eye. "I'll do it. If you want, I mean. We can go together and just tell me what to do to him." I knew he was serious, trying to help in a rather messed up way, so I told him I would think it over. It only took half a bottle of whiskey for me to decide. I couldn't see any way that I could feel worse at that moment, and I was certain that the guilt from killing Hayes would be nothing compared to the guilt I felt over Liz's death.

Retribution was a curious idea really, something the left wing (myself included) found abhorrent and morally inexcusable. Capital punishment was one thing but allowing relatives of victims to carry out the killing themselves seemed beyond wrong. But then the arguments for it became stronger with research. The society of psychiatrists and numerous mental health practitioners started displaying the benefits; how it could help with the grieving process, provide closure, relieve guilt. I could not foresee an end to the grief, and a large part of me did not want to stop grieving, but the guilt was the most unbearable. If I could feel as if I had avenged her death, then perhaps the guilt would become more manageable. And, as Darren pointed out repeatedly, he is going to die anyway.

"What if we fail?" I asked, beginning to slur from the alcohol. "Remember that guy that got killed?" I was referring to a case from the previous year, in which a man called Tom something had been granted retribution rights to kill the drink driver who had run over his toddler. The tables had turned and before the authorities could get into the room, Tom had his neck broken by the prisoner.

"That guy was an idiot," Darren said. "He untied the fucking guy. All we have to do is go in there and stab him. He'll be restrained; it's not a bloody gladiator fight." I was nervous, anxious. Darren seemed too confident, but I put this down to him being supportive rather than relishing the idea of killing another human being. I filled out the forms and had them sent back via email while I was still drunk enough to think it was a good idea.

Three days was all it took before we were being led into the holding ward, my palms sweaty, heart racing. I felt sick, the combination of nerves and uncertainty in what I was about to do starting to take over. I almost backed out, but I had put both myself and Darren on the form, and if I didn't go in, then he would probably go ahead without me, adding to my guilt instead of relieving it.

"The prisoner is restrained," we were told by a bored looking warden. He was a big guy, late forties probably, who appeared numb to the horrors of his job. "Under no circumstances are you to remove his restraints. There is a table to the side with some implements that you can use. We will have guards posted outside the room at all times, and we will be watching on these monitors." He nodded towards a trio of screens in front of him. On the screens, I saw Steven Hayes from three different angles, tied to a hospital bed, with two guards in the room awaiting our arrival. "You have fifteen minutes, so please don't drag it out." I wondered then if the cleaning up fell on to the guards, and whether this is why they seemed as if everything was a huge hassle for them.

The door opened with a loud buzz as the warden pressed a button under his desk. The two officers inside the room gave us a curt nod as they left, presumably to watch on the screens outside. Darren eyed the silver trolley with an inappropriate grin.

"This looks pretty savage," he declared, holding up a shiny meat cleaver. "You want to go first?" I turned to look at Hayes. He looked as if he had accepted his fate, staring at the ceiling through watery brown eyes.

"I don't think I can," I muttered, the nausea growing inside me.

"What are friends for?" Darren asked and before I could respond, he marched over to the side of the bed and slammed the cleaver into the man's shoulder. There was a scream as it went in deep, a spray of blood hitting Darren in the face. He looked crazed as he brought the cleaver down again on the shoulder, and again, until Steven's entire right arm hit the floor with a thud.

"Do you want to say anything to him?" Darren asked me. "If so, better do it soon. He looks like he might pass out." I approached the bed, slightly afraid, mostly angry. This was my primal moment, my chance for vengeance.

"Why did you do it?" was all I could ask. It was what I wanted to know above all else. "Was it meant to just be a burglary?" I could feel my eyes welling up, but I fought the tears back.

"I didn't," he said, facing me. "I didn't." For a second, there was a flicker of doubt in my mind as I looked at him. A moment that was interrupted by Darren bringing the cleaver down on his chest in a frenzy, crunching through ribs until bloody bubbles came through from his hacked-up lungs. I heard a final gush of air escape Steven Hayes' body as the life drained out of him, leaving a crimson mess staring at the ceiling once more. Then the sickness came. I bolted out of the room to find somewhere to vomit, greeted by the guards who simply pointed to a door to indicate the toilets. Darren came out a few minutes later. What I didn't know was that he had seized the moment when I left the room and the guards were briefly distracted, stealthily pulling his own knife from inside his workman's boots and slicing Hayes open along one side of his torso. On his way to putting the now-red cleaver back on the trolley, he casually carved a second notch in the knife's handle and hid it away.

One anonymous tip-off, he thought, giving one last glance at Hayes. That was all it took, and they were screaming for your blood.

Scratches

"What on earth are they doing now?" Angela asked me, becoming irritated that she could not get to sleep yet again. The new neighbours weren't especially noisy, but our bedrooms were only separated by one, seemingly thin, wall. In the month or so since they had moved in, we had heard all kinds of things and learned a lot about their routine from our position in bed, trying to get to sleep. One of them runs a bath at 10.45pm each day. There is often the muffled sound of conversation, which sometimes escalates to an argument. Once we could hear them having sex. *Only once, in almost five weeks,* I thought. *No wonder they don't sound happy.* The sound that was causing this evening's irritation was not talking, not shouting, and not even the groan of pipes as the bath water started to flow. It was scratching; a cross between the noise that one makes when stripping wallpaper with a scraper, and someone dragging fingernails across a rough surface.

"It's probably just mice," I said, immediately regretting it. Angela hates mice. She hates rodents of any kind, in fact, particularly if they are keeping her from sleeping.

"Then call pest control in the morning," she said, wedging her head in between her two pillows. I turned on to my side, my back facing Angela, and listened to the sound as it penetrated the darkness of our bedroom. *Scratch, scratch, scratch.* It was too quick to be the neighbour carrying out some home improvements; more like a scurrying sound. Like mice. I'd never had to use the pest-control people before, and money was tight, so I needed to be certain it was actually a problem. *Tomorrow I'll go next door and ask if they heard anything,* I decided, drifting off to the sound of unwelcome visitors in the skirting boards.

We overslept the following morning, rushing around to get out of the house on time and making no mention of Angela's pest-control demands. I didn't forget; I simply chose to put it off. It was too early in the morning to be knocking on doors, so I decided to wait until after work before speaking to our neighbours. *Or perhaps we should wait and see if we hear the sounds again tonight?* I was happy to ignore it but knew that Angela would become more and more irritated if I did not do something to fix the problem. Of course, any problems like this fell to me to deal with, being the man of the house. As much as Angela proclaimed to believe in equal rights regardless of gender, what she actually expected was that her man should do as she commanded; being needed was something that I usually enjoyed, despite there being times when it became a bit much.

I arrived home at my usual time, which provided me with one peaceful hour before Angela was due home. I took this opportunity to search online for prices for pest control, discovering that an initial visit and treatment program was way beyond my budget. *She won't be happy.* I climbed the stairs to our bedroom, unsure of what I expected to find, but needing to be able to show Angela I had taken her demands seriously. I stood in silence, closing my eyes, listening out for the scratching sound. Nothing. All I could hear was the sound of the traffic outside as rush hour entered full swing. Then a resounding crash from the other side of the wall, loud enough to startle me. I paused, unsure of what had caused it, but it was soon followed by the sobs of a small child and the muffled voice of her mother.

I gave the skirting boards a cursory glance over, checking for any visible signs of an infestation, of which there were none. *Maybe they were just wiping something off the walls? Perhaps the kid drew on them? If that's the case, then Angela can rest easy, and I've done my bit.* Hesitantly, I made my way back down the stairs and clicked the door on the catch. I stepped over the small wall which separated the two properties and gave the glass pane three sharp knocks. *I should have waited. What if the kid has broken something? They might not be in the mood to talk about rodents.* I cursed my own lack of confidence and waited for a little longer, before knocking again. This time I saw the pink shape of someone growing larger through the frosted glass and was greeted by my frantic looking neighbour.

"Hiya," she said, trying to hide her annoyance at the interruption.

"Hi," I replied. "Sorry to just come around like this."

"It's OK. Millie just pulled her chest of drawers over, so I was clearing that up." The woman, whose name I had never been told, looked frazzled; the constant need to supervise a child who was now at an inquisitive age clearly taking a toll.

"Yeah, I heard a bang. Is she alright?"

"Yes, just frightened her. Is that why you came around?" I paused, trying to think of the right words. It was nice that she thought I had been checking up on her daughter's safety, but I would have to admit that it wasn't really my reason for visiting.

"Sort of. Well, no, not really," I explained, awkwardly. "We heard a weird noise last night, like scratching, or scraping. About eleven o'clock. I just wanted to see if you'd been cleaning the walls, or scraping something? It's not a problem," I said quickly, frightened that it would seem as though I was complaining. "But Angela thinks we have mice in the skirting boards."

"Oh? No, we weren't doing anything like that. Can't say we heard anything, either. I was asleep before ten, but I can ask Mark when he gets home if you want?" Before I could say anything else, we were interrupted by shouts of 'mum' from upstairs, and I took that as my cue to leave.

"Not to worry then," I mumbled as the door closed in my face.

Angela had been home for less than five minutes before she asked how it had gone with the pest-control people. I looked at her with a confused expression. *Did she really think I took time off work, and been able to get them here so quickly?*

"They haven't been out yet," I said.

"Well, when are they coming?"

"I don't know. I didn't call them." I waited for her complaint, but she said nothing, choosing to simply stare at me and wait for me to elaborate. "I've been at work. But I did find the phone number and get a price online," I explained, hoping this would show that I had taken some steps towards dealing with it.

"I guess that's a start." Angela looked as if she wanted me to keep talking.

"And I went next door. They weren't scraping anything, but they didn't hear the noises either. I think we should see what happens tonight; if it happens again, I'll call someone out tomorrow." I had no idea how I would pay for it, but it went a small way to easing Angela's worries.

"OK. Make sure you do."

I desperately hoped that all would be quiet when bedtime came around, but it was worse than the night before. Even as we climbed the stairs, we could hear the sound of tiny scratches behind the wooden skirting boards. I dropped to my knees on the laminate flooring, listening intently as I tried to identify the cause. It was as if whatever was behind the glossed whiteness was trying to scratch its way out.

"It sounds trapped in there," I said, once again without thinking.

"Well I don't want something dying in the walls! It will stink the house out." Angela was right, as always.

"So, what do you suggest?" I was tired and growing impatient. I could see that our uninvited guests were about to cause a fight between us.

"You're going to have to take the skirting board off. It only seems to be this one wall." I looked at the floor, weighing up my words before I spoke. Removing the board itself would not be too difficult, and I was confident that I could do it with minimal damage. What put me off was the extremely heavy, five-door, mirrored wardrobe that was in the way.

"Fine," I replied. "But I'll need your help shifting this stuff out of the way." Angela looked at me in disbelief. She was about to protest but decided against it, instead offering to help move the wardrobe, so long as she could leave the room before I pulled the skirting away. Fifteen minutes later, we had piled most of the wardrobe's contents on to our bed and dragged it far enough from the wall to allow me to squeeze behind it. All the activity on our side of the wall must have panicked whatever was within it, and the sounds became louder, more intense, almost disturbing. *Scratch, scratch, scratch.* I told Angela to go and grab my toolbox, which she did without complaint. Once I had pulled a mallet and scraper out, she left me to it, hauling a spare duvet from the cupboard and announcing that she would be sleeping on the sofa. I looked at our bed, buried beneath piles of clothes, and knew it would be a late night.

I had no doubt by this point that it was mice. Or, perhaps, rats. The scratching sounds could be heard along the full length of the wall, and I started to grow concerned. *What if I expose a whole bloody nest? There could be hundreds of them in there! A mischief, that's what a group of mice or rats are called. Sounds about bloody right!* Cautiously, I banged the edge of the scraper into the corner of the skirting board, where the two adjacent pieces met. It was louder than I had expected, and I was worried about disturbing next door, but I was more worried about pissing off Angela. Whatever was inside became more frantic at the sound of the banging, desperate to be released. I repeated the action at the other corner, loosening the board at both ends, before starting along the top of the skirting. It was old and began to come away without too much difficulty. Once I had separated the top of the board from the wood along its entire length, something strange happened. The scratching sound, which had increased to a monumental racket up to this point, stopped. Suddenly, there was silence. I looked towards the bedroom door, debating whether or not to call Angela, but decided against it.

It was only as I grabbed the top of the wood that I noticed how fiercely my hands were trembling. *It's just some bloody mice,* I thought, at least trying to convince myself of that fact. The wood came away with a creak, splitting at the edges a little but largely in one piece. The gap was only a few inches, but the bedroom light was too weak to illuminate it, so I fumbled about in my toolbox for a torch. I shone it up and down the gap, the light bouncing around the cobwebs and woodlouse carcasses. Aside from a pair of large house spiders, the space was empty. I scratched at my cheek, puzzled. It made no sense, but I was relieved a swarm of rodents hadn't launched themselves at me and down the stairs.

The sight of the dark opening made me uncomfortable; perhaps it was just the mystery of it all. I was torn between fixing the board back into place and sleeping downstairs, but due to the lateness of the hour, it wasn't much of a choice. I closed the bedroom door, temporarily blocking the scene from my mind, and settled down on the second of our sofas. Angela stirred.

"All sorted?" she mumbled.

"Nothing in there," I told her. She rolled over to face me, almost slipping on to the floor. Her eyes opened a little.

"What was making that noise then?" she asked.

"Must have been next door, I guess. I'll go back around there tomorrow and speak to the guy. See if he knows anything." I tried my best to brush it off, to hide the dread I felt. Something wasn't right, but I needed to keep Angela from getting herself worked up.

I didn't sleep well, unable to get comfortable. Angela seemed to manage, a little to my annoyance. By four in the morning, and after only dozing on and off, I gave up and went upstairs to clear the bed, desperate to get a few hours' sleep before work. Grumpily, I threw enough of the clothes into a heap on the floor to clear my side of the bed and crawled in. I was straight out; I enjoyed three full hours of deep sleep before my alarm began to screech. *Nope, too tired,* I decided, certain that I could get away with calling in sick.

The only words I heard from Angela were 'I'm off', to which I mumbled a reply that she would not have been able to hear. I dozed for a large part of the morning, until there came a point at which I knew I had to drag myself out of bed and deal with the mess I had made. It was only as I reached down to scratch an itch on my leg that something felt off, sore even. I yanked away the duvet and recoiled at the sight, leaping into a sitting position and shuffling myself back against the headboard as though trying to distance myself from my own legs. From the edges of my underwear, all the way to my ankles, my legs were bright red with scratches. Angry lines covering the previously white and pasty flesh. Specks of dried blood dotted the sheet and the duvet cover, but most of the scratches had not broken the skin; it was just raised and reddened. The sight of it reminded me of how my back had looked on several occasions when Angela and I had started dating, and the lovemaking had been much more affectionate than it is now.

I couldn't get my head around it, no matter how hard I tried to come up with an explanation. It looked nothing like an allergic reaction, or heat rash, or even some rare medical condition. I had been furiously scratched, and yet had felt nothing.

It made no sense. I scoured the room for some indication as to what could have done this to me but there was nothing; no strands of fur, no tiny footprints, and definitely no horde of rabid mice. I wanted to call Angela, but realized with sadness that she would, most likely, think I was being silly. So instead I set about my tasks, applying wood glue along the skirting board and fixing it back into place. It wasn't a perfect job, but with a touch up of gloss, it was certainly passable. The wardrobe took all my strength to return it to its usual position, but I managed, within a couple of hours, to have the room looking just as it had done the previous day.

I still had not gotten dressed when Angela returned from work, parading about in an old T-shirt and yesterday's underwear. Any other time, she would have made a comment about laziness, or me being a slob, but she was too transfixed on the state of my legs to say anything derogatory.

"What the fuck have you been doing?" she asked, a little angrily, as if I had done this to myself. I explained that I had woken up like this, but that was all the explanation I could offer. I thought she would be frightened, but if she was, then she hid it well. Instead, she looked at me as though I was insane.

"I can't do this anymore," she told me. I must have looked as confused as I felt, standing there without speaking. I genuinely did not understand what she meant. "I don't know what's going on with you," she continued. "I only asked you to call a pest-control guy, and you've taken the wall apart, scratched your legs up, you're acting weird. It's like you can't manage a simple task without either doing it wrong or blowing it up into some huge drama." I still didn't understand where she was going with this. "I'm going to get some stuff and stay at my sister's house tonight. We'll talk in a few days." Finally, my mind processed what she had said.

"You're leaving me? Because something scratched my legs?" I shouted, emphasizing how ridiculous that was.

"Quick!" she called from our room. "That sound!" I ran up the stairs to find her, and she was right; the scratching sound was back.

"What the hell?" I wondered aloud.

"Seems pretty obvious to me," she stated, shoving some toiletries into an overnight bag. I stared at her, unable to see what she thought was so clearly a credible explanation. "You can't have looked properly. Some wild thing is in there and must have got to you when you left the board off. Which is *exactly* why I didn't want to sleep in here last night. It probably scurried back in, and now you've trapped it again. Fix it, then we'll talk about where we go from here." With that, she was gone down the stairs and out of the house with a slam of the front door. *Scratch, scratch, scratch.* Something took over me, a rage of some kind, I suppose. I was angry and hurt that Angela could use such a feeble excuse to leave, fed up with the constant criticism from her, disappointed in my own ability to resolve simple problems. Like this fucking scratching. *Scratch, scratch, scratch.*

Angrily, I pulled at the wardrobe, now refilled and heavy, managing to drag it barely six inches from the wall. I kicked at the skirting with my bare feet, which did not damage to the wood but sent a bolt of pain up my leg. I screamed and dropped to the floor. *Scratch, scratch, scratch.* At that moment,

I did not care about preserving the skirting board; I had no forethought about the repair job I would need to perform. I wanted that sound to stop, and quickly. Frantically, I pulled a hammer from the toolbox and swung it at the wood, causing it to crack. The sound became louder; *scratch, scratch, scratch.* I hit it again, in the same spot. Pieces of wood splintered off, the start of an opening. I struck again and again, moving along the board until I had an opening about a foot long.

Once more, I shone the torch inside and saw nothing but cobwebs and dust. I placed my hands through the hole, gripping the board firmly, and heaved it away, re-opening the entire length just as it had been last night. Nothing scurried out; I was greeted only by silence. Using the hammer, I scraped around in the dark, pulling away the webs. Until I hit something. It wasn't something hard, not wood nor brickwork, but soft and living judging by the hiss it let out. I should have moved back, but my rage was in full control; I needed to get the job done, to prove myself to Angela. I reached for the torch and shone it at the place the hammer rested, my face against the floor. Eyes stared back at me; two deep yellow eyes, not dissimilar to a cat's eyes.

But cats do not have hands; long fingered, withered, grey hands. They tapped their way across the floor towards me before I could react, grabbing my face on both sides. The eyes became larger as they came closer to my own, but the creature's face was hidden in the darkness. For what felt like far too long, we stared at each other, before I tried to pull myself back. I'd lost my strength, or this thing was not as frail as it appeared, and I could not fight it off. Dragged by the head, it took me into its darkness, my eyes and nose filling with dust and rancid cobwebs. I tried to scream but no sound came, only silence. I could not move, fixed into place by the brickwork and the creature, as I felt its fingernails run along my cheeks. My breathing became faster, more panicked, as I tasted the salty skin entering my mouth, fingers exploring the inside of my cheeks. Then, swiftly, there was a sudden bolt of pain as my mouth filled with blood. I tried to spit it out but could not. My eyes widened with terror as I realized that my freshly removed tongue was now blocking my airways.

The police ruled it as 'death by misadventure' after Angela reported it three days later. Of course, she had not heard from me since walking out, which no doubt only enraged her further, and had returned to find out why. And there I was; head rammed into the gap where the skirting board had been, sharp tools all around me and, despite no-one being able to explain how I had actually done it, I had apparently accidentally cut off my own tongue and choked on it. Death by misadventure, or death by stupidity as Angela called it. It took a few days for her to return home, having arranged for the board to be replaced whilst she pretended to grieve at her sister's house. And then it only took a few hours for the sounds to start again; *scratch, scratch, scratch.*

Trick or Treat

"You're all too old to go trick or treating," Mum had told us. "Leave it this year; let the little kids get the sweets. It's not as if Tommy needs to eat any more junk!" She was right about everything, of course. We were too old, and Tommy was already heading for a heart attack at the age of fifteen, his diet consisting largely of sausage rolls and fizzy drinks.

"We're still children," I replied, with a smile. "One last time, I promise. Anyway, it's all arranged and I'm meeting some people." I gave mum the innocent look that she could rarely refuse.

"What people?" she asked, studying my face to see if I was about to lie to her.

"Just Chloe and Phoebe. Tommy is walking over with them."

"Like a double date?" she asked, not looking as though she approved. She was strict and was convinced that any time I would spend time with a girl would end up with her becoming a grandmother.

"Just friends," I told her, and that was the truth, much to my disappointment. I liked both the girls, and so did Tommy. The difference between us was that Tommy didn't stand a chance with either of them, which made things a bit awkward. After muttering something about being safe and not getting up to any mischief, she finally relented and gave her reluctant blessing. Before she could finish laying down the rules, I was already on my way upstairs to get into my costume; a Grim Reaper outfit, complete with a mask and plastic scythe. As a test run, I decided to creep up behind my eight-year-old sister, who cried, so I guess it was sufficiently scary for the evening. I picked up my pumpkin-shaped plastic bucket which we had used for years to collect the treats in and told Mum that I was about to leave.

"Have you got your phone?" she asked.

"Nowhere to put it," I explained, running my hands down the sides of the costume to confirm the lack of pockets. "They are meeting me at the end of the road in a few minutes."

"And what if you need to call me?"

"I'm sure they will have phones with them, but we'll be fine." Mum looked worried. She always looked worried.

"OK, back at eight-thirty. That's late enough to be knocking on stranger's doors."

"Nine?" I asked, cheekily.

"Eight forty-five, and not a minute after." I lifted my mask to give her a peck on the cheek and ran out of the house, my black costume flapping behind me.

Tommy and the girls all lived on the same road, about a ten-minute walk from me. Without wanting to sound snobbish, it is a fact that my house is on the nicer side of town. This is why we planned to knock on doors near mine; apparently, some of the houses over their way weren't very friendly. This also made things easier with my Mum, knowing that I would be close by. I stood at the corner of the road feeling a little foolish in my costume, waiting for the others who were late as always. The thinness of the material provided little barrier against the cold wind, and I shivered, beginning to get impatient. I tried to construct a logical route in my head that would reap the most reward, but my thoughts were quickly interrupted by the sound of giggling coming from behind me. Tommy was wearing his usual clothes; blue jeans and a football shirt which did not completely cover his belly. The extent of his Halloween efforts consisted of some white face paint with a couple of red lines, which I presumed to represent blood.

The girls, on the other hand, had put in a lot of effort, and I was thankful that mum had not seen them. They wore matching, white nurses' uniforms. Their faces were painted green and looked zombie-like; I guess girls are good at the face paint and make-up side of things. Far better than Tommy, anyway. The uniforms were short, almost up to their buttocks, and red, fishnet stockings did little to cover the exposed flesh. I tried not to stare, but it wasn't easy.

"Where do you want to start?" I asked. "I thought we'd do my road and then the houses up towards the church; they're usually pretty good." The others laughed, looking at each other as if they had a secret. "What?" I asked, not understanding what was funny.

"The girls want to check out the Monroe house," Tommy stated, a mischievous grin on his face. He knew how I'd respond.

"Are you serious?" I asked, looking at the girls.

"Don't be a baby," Phoebe replied, taking my hand. As much as it felt like a terrible idea, peer-pressure and a pretty girl made my mind up for me. The Monroe house was isolated, being situated on the edge of a large, green, public space, out of sight of any other houses. Dog walkers were pretty much the only people to ever pass the house, and rarely after dark. At this time of the year, the Monroe house went all-out for Halloween, with elaborate decorations adorning the front garden and exterior of the house. None of us had met anyone who had actually seen someone living at the house, and this had sparked a range of playground rumours. Of course, the house was haunted, no-one dared to refute that out loud (although I doubted that it was the case). Only Max, a boy from school who was in the year above us, claims to have been there last Halloween.

"You don't actually believe Max's nonsense about knocking there before, do you?" I said, as we made our way past rows of terraced houses with pumpkins in the windows.

"It's probably bullshit," Tommy said, starting to feel a little nervous as we approached the darkness of the dirt track.

"Yeah, maybe. In which case there's no harm having a look," Phoebe said, squeezing my hand. "And what if he was telling the truth?" Max's version, which is highly debatable, was that he had knocked on the door of the Monroe house, bravely by himself, calling out trick or treat. Although he didn't see anyone, Max told everyone around the school that some wrinkly fingers with long nails had pushed a fifty-pound note out of the letter box. He had stood staring at it in disbelief when the three full-sized skeletons that were decorating the garden turned to face him. He insists that they chased him away, and as much as everyone laughed at him, no-one dared to go there and find out for themselves. Hence, the legend began.

Part of me hoped the house would not have been decorated, that the lights would be off, that we would decide not to knock. I'm sure we all gasped a little as we turned the corner from the track and gazed upon the Monroe house. Three plastic skeletons were erected in the garden, positioned with shovels around a hole in the ground. A hole which looked to be the right size to bury a body. There were tacky decorations in all the front-facing windows; strings of lights with ghosts and pumpkins, decals of witches on the glass, and a light-up sign attached to the front door which read 'enter if you dare!'.

"It looks pretty cool," Chloe said.

"Guess so," I muttered, my eyes fixed on the skeletons, just in case they moved. Which they didn't, of course.

"Give the door a knock then," Tommy ordered, from his position about six feet behind the rest of us. "Let's get this fifty quid, and we'll go somewhere else." I looked at him as if he were an idiot. We were gathered by the small gate which opened on to the property, no-one wanting the take the lead. After a series of awkward glances had been exchanged, Chloe huffed and walked through the gate.

"If no-one else comes to the door, then the money is all mine," she stated, turning to face us. Again, Phoebe gripped my hand tighter and followed her friend toward the door, dragging me with her. Chloe banged on the door; three loud knocks echoed throughout the house. We were greeted by silence.

"No-one home," I declared with relief, turning to leave. Chloe knocked again. This time we heard footsteps, accompanied by a kind of dragging sound; the first image to come to mind was a heavy-set person dragging a body. We all took a step back and waited, suddenly hopeful that some money would be pushed through the letterbox after all. However, it wasn't; the only sound was that of numerous locks being undone. I wanted to leave at this point, but I was also frightened to run away after we had disturbed whoever lived there.

When the last locked clicked, there was a pause. I wondered if the resident was elderly and had changed their mind about opening the door. Then, with a creak, it began to swing open.

"Trick or treat," Chloe announced, trying to sound friendly. There was no-one there, just a dark hallway barely illuminated by a string of fairy lights of either side. "Hello?" she called into the house.

"Probably a good time to leave," I said, no longer caring if my friends thought I was a wimp. There was no-one there and walking in would be trespassing.

"Hello?" Chloe called again, this time placing one foot across the threshold.

"You can come in!" came a voice, startling us all. It sounded as though it belonged to an old woman.

"Sorry if we disturbed you," I called in response, whispering to the others once again that we should leave.

"It's no bother," the voice replied. "I've got some Halloween treats here, if that is what you were after? Just in the hallway, help yourself. Sorry I can't bring them out; I'm a bit frail these days."

"See! It's fine," Chloe said, not sounding entirely convinced.

"Seriously?" Tommy said, a little more loudly than he had intended. "She could make it to the door to open it, so why didn't she bring the treats then?" He had a point. The temptation of money, or even some other decent reward got the better of us and each holding on to one another, we crept into the hallway.

"Leave the door open," I told Tommy, who looked at me as if to say that was the most obvious thing in the world.

"I've set up a Halloween game in the hallway if you want to play?" asked the voice. "Do a trick, get a treat. I hope you enjoy it." It was creepy, and I was beyond having second thoughts. I decided that we should see the Monroe woman, at least show our faces, so I walked into the dark room that the voice came from.

"Hello?" No reply. I fumbled for a light switch. It didn't work.

"The power must be off," Tommy suggested.

"The fairy lights are working," I said, pointing to the plug sockets that they were attached to.

"Bulb must have gone, then," he said.

"Hello?" I called again, moving further into the room. Nothing. My eyes adjusted to the dark a little and there was no doubt that the room was empty. I felt colder. Something was wrong. "I'm going," I told them, turning back towards the door. Before anyone could answer me, the door slammed shut, the bolts' locking of their own accord. Chloe screamed. Phoebe began to cry.

"What the fuck?" Tommy declared. He ran to the door, attempting to pull back the bolts but found them to be red hot; the tips of two fingers and his thumb now blistered. "Fucking hell!"

"I don't like this," Phoebe said, between sobs.

"Call someone," I suggested. "I left my phone at home." The three of them all pulled their phones out of bags and pockets. No signal on any of them; not phone signal or Internet coverage. The only option for us was to look for another way out. From the outside, we saw two large windows on the ground floor, with the hallway being central to the house. The living room that we had investigated was on our left; there should have been a door to the right, but the wall was solid. There were three, front-facing windows on the first floor, but we could not see any stairs as we approached the end of the hallway. It was dark, but I could sense the dread that the others were feeling, hear the sobs that Phoebe tried to stifle.

"We'll have to smash the living room window and climb out," Tommy suggested, his voice rising in panic. Unable to think of anything else, we walked back along the corridor only to discover that there was now no door on either side. We returned to the entrance, to find the locks still white-hot. We were trapped, completely walled in. Chloe flicked on the flashlight app on her phone. The only items in the hallway were two boxes, each about two feet cubed. One was labelled *tricks*; the other was labelled *treats*. Tommy opened the treats' box as Chloe shone her light into it. It was empty. Cautiously, the pair opened the tricks' box. There were five black envelopes in the box, each numbered, beginning at one. Tommy picked up the first and opened it, pulling the card from inside. As he read it, he couldn't help smiling and, for a brief moment, I thought everything was going to be OK.

"What's it say?" I asked.

"It says," Tommy began, "that when we complete the trick card, we will get a treat card."

"But the box was empty."

"Yeah, well the bloody living room was there a moment ago."

"And what is the trick?"

"It says we have to kiss each other." Tommy was smirking.

"Oh, piss off!" Phoebe said. "You're making that up. It's hardly the time for joking about." Tommy showed us the card, and he was right; 'Kiss the other members of your group'. It sounded simple enough. We all looked at each other, a little uneasily. Then Phoebe kissed me, full on the mouth. My teenage brain kicked in, and I kissed her back, not wanting to waste the opportunity. When she eventually pulled away, we looked at Tommy and Chloe. He wore a huge grin, but she looked as though she would vomit.

"It'll be fine," Phoebe told her, as if trying to prepare her for an unpleasant ordeal. They kissed, awkwardly and quickly, before opening the treats' box once again. Empty.

"I read the card, so maybe I have to kiss both of you," Tommy said, winking at Phoebe in the dark. She didn't hesitate, and having nothing better to suggest, kissed him on the mouth. Still no treat, unless you count the pleasure Tommy was getting from it all.

"Or maybe you have to kiss *everyone*," Chloe suggested, looking a little pleased with herself. It took me a moment to realize what she meant.

"Nope!" I said, without hesitation.

"It's no more gross than us having to kiss him," Chloe told me.

"Thanks!" Tommy replied. "Come here, big boy!" he said to me, trying to make light of the situation.

"OK, but no tongues," I warned him. He didn't listen, finding the whole thing funny as he slipped his tongue into my mouth. I leapt back in disgust. Chloe was right. He had needed to kiss us all, and there was now a treat envelope to open.

"Ten pounds," Tommy announced as he pulled it from the envelope and stuffed it into his pocket.

"To split," Chloe said.

"It was my card!" he retorted.

"You were the only one enjoying it; we should be paid for having to kiss you!"

"Like a prostitute?" Tommy replied, smugly. Chloe stopped talking after that.

"We can worry about that if we get out of here. Who is going to open the second trick?"

"I'll do another," Tommy offered. "Maybe I'll get a hand-job this time."

"I'd rather die," Chloe said. "I'll do it." Handing the phone to Tommy to hold, she read the second card aloud. "Slap the other members of your group." With an idea of the rules, and no restraint, Chloe smacked Tommy across the face, hard. He yelped and looked angry but kept his mouth shut. She proceeded to slap me, not with much force, and then Phoebe, muttering an apology as she did it. Quickly, she turned to the treats' box and pulled out the new envelope, stuffing the twenty-pound note into the top of her stockings.

"Now you really look like a whore," Tommy told her. She ignored him. "Who's next?" He looked at Phoebe and me. I let her choose and, with the assumption that the tricks would become more severe, she asked to go next. After I had nodded, she opened the box, taking out the third envelope and reading it in her head. Her eyes widened a little, and she looked at us nervously.

"I'm not doing that," she said, holding the card to her chest. "Let's check the door again, maybe we can touch the locks with something over our hands?"

"Like what?" Tommy asked. "You two are pretty much naked and that Grim Reaper outfit looks like it'd burst into flames." Phoebe headed to the door regardless, and we heard a clink as she slid one of the bolts aside. I ran over to her in excitement.

"Have they cooled down?"

"Only the bottom two. You can feel the heat from the other four."

"Two cards, two locks," I muttered as our eyes met. "We're going to have to do all of them."

"But there are five cards and six locks," she pointed out.

"Maybe the last treat is the final bolt?" I said, hopefully. "What did your card say?" She passed it to me and looked at the floor. 'Take blood from the other members of your group'. Attached to the card with some tape was a razor blade.

"It's fine," I told her, putting my hands on her shoulders. "I'm sure just a drop will be enough; it won't hurt." I unstuck the blade and handed it to her, extending my fingers in front of her. "Just prick the end." It stung like a paper cut, quickly turning crimson as a few drops fell from the end of my forefinger. Tommy and Chloe were still bickering and hadn't heard what we needed to do. Perhaps the strangeness of the situation had gotten to them, but they did not try to refuse. After all, what else could we have done. Phoebe went to the door to check our theory out and found three bolts were now cool enough to handle. In the treat box was an envelope containing a fifty-pound note.

"I guess I'm up next," I said, moving towards the box.

"Shit, sorry," Tommy mumbled, holding card number four in his hands. "I've just read it." He didn't look happy. I snatched it from him; 'Choose one member of the group to leave behind'.

"Well I don't see what you're meant to do, it's not as if we can get out yet," I told him.

"And we aren't leaving anyone behind!" Chloe said, panicking that Tommy would choose her. I opened the treat box but found nothing. We were puzzled, not understanding what was required of us.

"Just pick someone and say the words," Phoebe suggested. "As long as we all understand that we don't really leave anyone here." We all nodded.

"I choose Chloe to leave behind," Tommy announced, loudly. Chloe slapped him for a second time, muttering *prick* under her breath. "Easy money," Tommy said, tearing at the fourth envelope. "This is becoming quite profitable," he said, holding up eighty pounds with a greedy grin. He added the money to his earlier 'prize', and then it happened. Perhaps it was a delay from him saying the words, maybe it needed him to actually pocket the cash, but that was confirmation enough. A swirling pattern began to appear on the wall behind Chloe. Before we could warn her, six arms reached out as far as the elbow, wrapping around our friend. She let out a muffled scream, but it was too late; they pulled her into the wall, and she was gone. Too quickly for us to react, too suddenly for us to even process what was happening. Phoebe launched herself at Tommy, pounding his huge gut with punches. He felt responsible, that much was obvious, but she was gone and there was no obvious way to get her back.

"One more card," I said. "Let's get this done and get out. We can find help once we escape this house." I picked up the final card, ignoring my apprehension. I just wanted this to be over with. Inside the envelope was a small rubber stamp and ink; the sort of thing you find in gift shops at tourist attractions. I opened it to see a skull design. 'Choose one member of the group to play with the skeletons.'

"That doesn't sound like something any of us want to do," Phoebe said. "Remember Max said those things in the garden chased him."

"If that's the case, then I should choose myself; I'm most likely to be able to outrun them."

"What if you can't? Or if that isn't what it means?" We both looked at Tommy.

"Do whatever," he said, not seeming to care. "If those bony fuckers try anything then I'll sit on them." He was trying to sound brave, but his voice quivered as he spoke. It was selfish of me, but he had done that to Chloe, so it felt fair. If I had to choose between Tommy and Phoebe, then there was no choice at all. I walked over and stamped a red skull on Tommy's forehead.

"That was the last card," I pointed out, opening the treats' box. There was a larger envelope; thick and padded. From inside I pulled out a card with a grinning clown, and a thick glove. I stared at it for a moment. *Heatproof,* I told myself, slipping it on. We ran to the door, pulling across the last of the bolts and yanking it open. Outside was dark, but nothing like what we had been enclosed within. As we stepped into the fresh air, our path was blocked by the grave-digging skeletons, heads cocked to one side as they surveyed us. We froze, just for a moment. Then something registered with them as they seemed to notice the stamp on Tommy's head. It happened in the briefest of moments; he was surrounded and all three, simultaneously, extended their bony hands. They jabbed at Tommy's belly with such speed that they became a blur, the white bones turning red in the spray.

Tommy's eyes were wide, his mouth gurgling blood as he dropped to the ground. We didn't try to help him, it was too late, so we ran. Phoebe and I, together, leaving our friend to be dragged into the freshly dug earth.

The house was deserted when we came back with help. There were no decorations, no old lady, just dust and empty rooms. The doors were where they should have been, as were the stairs. It was as if nothing had happened, and it was just us playing a Halloween prank. Of course, Chloe and Tommy were never found, and we were under scrutiny regarding their disappearances, but no-one could prove anything. The only person that believed us was Max, who had actually had company when he visited the Monroe house last year but had been too afraid to mention the disappearance of his older brother. A year later and Max's parents still think their oldest child is travelling the world.

Tunnels

Ghost hunters. Just another group of fraudsters along with psychics, witch doctors and faith healers. As much as I enjoyed a good scary story, I had no doubts that this was all it was; just a story. Even so, fear had an appeal; the adrenalin was addictive. Between my wife and I, we had seen almost every horror film worth watching, and many that weren't. We'd read countless tales of vengeful ghosts, demonic possession, psychotic killers, and zombie infestations. Then came the immersive experiences which have exploded in popularity over the past few years.

Our first was a Halloween horror show on a farm; essentially a walk-through filled with actors whose job it was to terrify the visitors. This initial experience blew us away, leaving us desperate for more. We attended theatrical murder mystery events and frightening team games, which involved solving puzzles to escape 'certain death'. We screamed our way through the city's old dungeons, and even attended a weekend of 'zombie outbreak survival' training.

It became a hobby, of sorts, and we were constantly searching for the next horrifying experience. Sometimes we would drive for hours to try out a new attraction, listening to creepy audio books on the journey to set the mood. We'd been face-to-face with killer clowns, living scarecrows, and more than a handful of zombies. We'd been startled by bumps in the night and had literally run away from a chainsaw-wielding maniac. The only thing that did not hold any interest, to me at least, were ghosts. Pretend ghostly effects were fine; what I could not understand were events which claimed to be able to show you real ghosts. Confident in my belief that they did not exist, I saw no appeal in spending the night being guided down damp passageways, only to have my beliefs confirmed, and to have to pay for the privilege.

My wife, however, had always believed in ghosts; which may explain why she usually found these things more frightening than I did, and why after a particularly well-done ghost film, she would need me to accompany her to the bathroom, turning on every light on the way. She was regularly pointing out these ghost-hunting events, and I was invariably ignoring her not-so-subtle hints; until one came up at a venue within walking distance of our home. The poster invited people to explore 'the famously haunted tunnels of the wartime fort', a structure which was, perhaps, a mile from our house at most. We had visited the fort on numerous occasions, to look around the museum and enjoy a coffee, but we had never been there after dark.

"Famously haunted?" I said, with a disapproving look. "Can't be that famous."

"We have to go!" Lily demanded, a serious look on her face. "Plus, you owe me for that last place we went to."

"What place?" I asked, despite knowing full-well what she meant. It was advertised with all the usual buzzwords; terrifying, shocking, horrific and so on. But it was also being touted as 'next-level'; claiming previous visitors had left screaming as it was just 'too intense'. Unfortunately, it turned out to simply be a field in the middle of nowhere, full of terrible actors running around, struggling not to laugh themselves. I smiled at the memory; it had been so awful that it now seemed funny. Lily did not agree, and just looked at me. I sighed.

"Fine. On one condition."

"Hmm?"

"If we don't find any ghosts, then we don't go on another ghost hunt again."

"OK, deal."

"And..." I continued. "And we find a secluded bit of the tunnels to get frisky in." There was a pause as I waited for Lily to laugh my suggestion off, but she didn't.

"I'll wear a skirt then," she announced, a coy smile appearing on her red lips.

When the day arrived, I did not feel anything like my normal level of enthusiasm. I was more tired than usual, and the thought of going through empty tunnels until three in the morning on a cold, drizzly night was not at all appealing.

"You still want to go tonight?" I asked.

"Of course. I can't wait!" Lily replied. "Don't be wimping out on me now."

"I'm not. It's just going to be a late one, and I'm tired already."

"So, have a nap before we go. I'm still going, even if you don't come. And if you still want this..." Lily said, lifting her skirt high enough to reveal the black lace beneath. I gasped, involuntarily.

"I can't say no to that," I told her, trying to shift the reluctant feeling I had about the evening. I was not tired enough to sleep during the day, but spent the afternoon lounging on the sofa, watching old vampire films from the 1960s while Lily pottered around the house.

"Should we take anything with us?" she asked, popping her head around the living room door. It was getting dark outside, and I still had little motivation to move from where I lay.

"Like what?"

"I don't know. I have the tickets in my bag, but wondered if we should take torches? Or drinks?"

"Both would be good; I suppose. Even just for getting back afterward, a torch would be useful; it's a dark walk from the fort to the main road in the middle of the night. Will you be warm enough in that skirt?"

"I'll be fine. I'll take a hat and coat - you should do the same." Lily walked out of the room, leaving me to continue staring at the television, watching as a vampire sank his teeth into the neck of young virgin, all played out in black and white. Soon, Lily returned carrying two torches. She clicked them both on at the same time, right into my eyes.

"Jesus!" I muttered.

"They work!" she declared. "And I have spare batteries in my bag. Get yourself ready, it's almost time!" she squealed, barely able to hide her excitement. As I pulled on my walking boots, Lily handed me a water bottle. I stared at the bubbles drifting to the surface.

"It's fizzy," I pointed out, dryly.

"Gin and tonic. It is Friday night, after all."

Linking arms, we made our way out into the cool air of the small town. It was peaceful outside, but with enough of a chill for our breath to become visible as we exhaled. The air felt damp, not really raining, but wet enough to make Lily's bare legs glisten with goose bumps. Despite it being Friday evening, the town was small, and we barely passed anyone else on the fifteen-minute walk to the fort. I glanced at my watch; it was eight thirty-five and we were almost there.

"We're going to be early," I pointed out.

"Better than being late. Plus, the tour starts at nine; we don't want to miss anything."

"How on earth is it going to take six hours to walk around the tunnels? The place isn't that big!"

"I suppose," Lily said with a smirk, "that it depends on what we find down there!"

"Probably nothing," I muttered. Either Lily didn't hear me, or she chose to ignore my negativity, but she did not respond. As we turned away from the main road on to the path which led up to the fort's entrance, Lily began to rummage through her bag for the torches. It was cold, and I was growing impatient.

"How much crap have you got in there?" I moaned, knowing all too well that her bag was like a bottomless pit, filled with an eclectic mix of supposedly essential items.

"Here we go," she announced, passing me one of the torches. "Let's go get spooked!" I smiled a little at her childlike enthusiasm, as she stood in front of me with her torch pointing upwards beneath her chin, illuminating her pretty face. She looked as though she were about to tell a scary story around a campfire.

"I'm just here for the black lace," I told her, giving her bottom a playful squeeze.

"Then you'd better not let the poltergeists get to me first!" We made our way up the path, thick trees forming a barrier on either side of us. It was dark, but the light from the almost-full moon would have nearly sufficed if we had had no torches. Barely twenty feet from the gated entrance, we heard the first scream of the evening; a high-pitched squeal of someone genuinely petrified. We both paused for a moment until we heard laughter following it. I sighed with relief, assuming that someone already inside had fallen victim to a prank of some kind. At least, I hoped that was what had happened.

We were greeted at the gates by the two organizers; Matthew and Chloe. They wore matching hooded tops, which bore the details of their business. I took this as evidence, if any were even needed, that this was purely a money-making venture. Of course, all the immersive events we had attended were businesses of some kind, but they never pretended to be anything other than that. These guys were trying to peddle some truth behind their ghost stories, and that was what had my back up.

Matthew was short, or Chloe was tall; it was difficult to tell from our position on the other side of the gate, in the dark. Either way, they were the same height. They were also both a little overweight and wore nearly identical glasses. In the blackness of the evening, it would have been quite possible to mistake one of them for the other, especially in their matching, branded, baseball caps. I wondered for a moment if they were siblings, or lovers. Then I pondered the idea that they were both, and I felt a little queasy.

"Good evening ghost hunters!" Matthew said, much more loudly than was necessary. The pair of them had unsettling grins across their faces, signalling, to me anyway, that we were about to be taken for a ride by these over-confident fraudsters.

"So, you've got ghosts here then?" I asked, making no attempt to hide my scepticism. Lily nudged me, as if I were embarrassing her already. As our guides removed the padlocked chain and proceeded to open up the wrought-iron gates, Lily pulled out the ticket confirmation that I had printed that morning. Once they had scrutinized the tickets, Matthew and Chloe welcomed us to what they promised would be 'a truly terrifying tour of one of the south coast's most haunted locations' and led us to the open space at the centre of the fort. Neither of them had answered my question about ghosts, barely seeming to acknowledge that I had even spoken. I was certain that I had offended them already, but did not particularly care; after all, I was on the gin and knew they were running a scam. Which is why I asked again.

"Is it just the one ghost? Or is there a whole family down there?" Chloe looked me in the eye, the grin falling away from her face, realizing that she was being mocked.

"There is no doubt that there are at least three spirits dwelling in the deeper tunnels, directly beneath where we are standing right now. It is quite possible that there are more. Hopefully, you will get to meet some of them tonight." Before I could respond, Chloe turned away and taking Matthew by the hand, the pair climbed on to a lone picnic table which stood outside of the small, now closed, coffee shop.

"Welcome everybody," Matthew began. There was a faint murmur from the other patrons. I looked around and counted another five people, beside myself and Lily. They had all been talking together when we had approached so it was impossible to tell if they had booked as one group or simply struck up a conversation on arrival.

"Before we begin, I need to go over some ground rules for everyone's safety," Matthew said, his voice beginning to sound more theatrical. "In the case of an emergency, the only exit is through the gates which you came in by. It was a working fort at one time and would therefore have been rather foolish to feature emergency exits!" He laughed a little at what he saw as his clever joke. No-one else laughed. "Anyway, the gates are currently locked, but both me and Chloe have keys; feel free ask either of us if you need to leave before the end." The gin was starting to go to my head, and the guy stood on the picnic table was irritating me, so I decided to ask a question.

"What if something happens to both of you, and we can't get the keys to get out?"

"I can assure you that won't be an issue," Matthew said with a smile. "We have dealt with many spirits in the past, some of which were rather aggressive, and we would not put any of you, or ourselves, in real danger."

"Of course," I muttered sarcastically.

"It is imperative," Matthew continued, "that we all stay together. I will take the lead, and Chloe will take up the rear." I sniggered, immaturely. Lily nudged me again. "You are welcome to take photographs, and we have extra torches if anyone needs one," our guide explained. "It is, of course, very dark in the tunnels and there are a lot of steep steps. Before I pass over to Chloe for a bit of history on the place, does anyone need to use the toilet?" No-one spoke. "Very well. Chloe will explain the legend of the haunting here, and then we'll be on our way."

"I'm going for a wee," I whispered to Lily, as soon as Chloe began speaking.

"OK."

"Wanna come?" I asked. Her eyes widened in mock surprise.

"I'm fine, thanks. Don't worry, you'll get your chance later with me. Now shh, I want to hear the story." With a little huff, I made my way back to the iron gates, next to which were the toilets. I dawdled as best I could, managing to miss the first half of Chloe's speech much to my relief. As I resumed my position next to Lily, I was just in time to hear about the three spirits which were supposedly haunting the tunnels.

"She had been a powerful witch, strong enough to place Henry Oats, a wealthy landowner, under her spell. He owned the land on which we are standing now, with his wife Clara, and daughter Elizabeth. The story goes that Henry was seduced by the witch, and caught in the act of lovemaking, by his wife. Clara was devastated, fleeing from the family home, only to be crushed to death outside by a falling oak. Was it a freak accident, or was it witchcraft?" Chloe looked at our small gathering, as if expecting an answer.

"Was it windy that night?" I asked. "Trees do blow over." I heard someone giggle from the other group, but Chloe chose to continue her tale.

"It was a still night, with no wind or any record of a storm." Chloe stared at me as she said this.

"She's just made that bit up," I whispered to Lily, who ignored me.

"Of course, no-one could prove that the witch was responsible for Clara's death, but there were suspicions among the locals. Henry seemed to take his wife's passing well, quickly moving his new lover into his home, enrolling her as a stepmother to little Elizabeth. The child had only been five years old when her mother had died, but she suspected foul play. Unable to understand her father's obsession with this strange woman, and his indifference to her mother's death, Elizabeth eventually sought help from officials in the nearest town. Despite the oddness of Clara's death, Elizabeth's concerns were chalked up to simply disliking her stepmother. This was until people started dying. Over the space of a year, there were a number of other freak accidents; falling trees, unexplained drownings, a shock suicide, and even the unfortunate case of a rich widow falling face-first into a fire. It did not take much digging to find a link between each of the newly deceased; they had all owned land which bordered onto Henry's or was very near to it. They had all, also, refused to sell it to him. Once this connection was established, the townsfolk were up in arms, angry, and thirsty for revenge. Henry was sleeping when the mob descended on his house, but Elizabeth was at the door, ready to let them in. The mob would not wait for a trial, fearful that the witch would use magic to escape, and she was sentenced to death by fire as soon as they had dragged her into the town square. Henry stayed at the house, powerless to help the woman, unwilling to watch her death in person. Elizabeth, however, wanted to see for herself that the witch was gone. Standing barely six feet away, her eyes met the witch's. Elizabeth watched the flames, oblivious to the cart behind her. She did not see its wheel hit a hole in the road, causing a barrel to fall. She did not see that barrel roll at her from behind. All she felt was herself falling forward into the flames. No-one from the crowd dared try to pull her out, too afraid that the barrel of gunpowder would explode." Chloe paused, perhaps in an attempt to create drama.

"And did it?" one of the girls called out.

"Yes, it did. The witch and Elizabeth were killed instantly. Shall we begin the tour?"

"Hang on," the girl called out again, an almost finished cigarette in her gloved hand. She was a little older than us, with dyed black hair, long dark coat, black lipstick, the works. "So, what happened to Henry?"

"No-one knows for sure," Chloe said. "He became a recluse, presumably devastated by the loss of his family. He died at the house, but there is no cause of death listed in the records."

"So, you're saying the three spirits here are Henry, Elizabeth and the witch? What about Clara? And the other people that the witch killed?" the goth woman asked.

"Perhaps they're all down there!" Matthew interjected. "Elizabeth likes to run along the narrow corridors, singing." At this point, Lily held my arm, a look of wonder on her face.

"I hope we get to see a ghost!" she whispered, excitedly.

"Let's hope it's Henry then," I told her, going along with the story. "Kids creep me out at the best of times, and that witch sounds like a right bitch!"

Matthew and Chloe led us to a door in the northeast corner of the fort; the entrance to a system of narrow tunnels which connected the various rooms. When the fort had been in use during the second world war, these rooms had been used to store ammunition and supplies for the soldiers stationed there. Once the door had been closed behind us, something which felt unnecessary, it was beyond simply being dark. It was now pitch black and if we had not had the torches, we would not have been able to see someone standing right in front of us. Lily clung on to me as we made our way down the first set of steep, concrete steps, half-expecting an actor to jump out on us at any moment. There was nothing. Our guides led us to the left as we reached the bottom of the steps, into a small room with candle-powered lanterns adorning the walls.

"If everyone can take a seat please, we will make our first attempt to establish contact with any spirits present, before we move on any farther," Matthew ordered. I looked across at the row of plastic, green chairs lined against one wall; eight of them. In front of the chairs stood a table with a Ouija board on it. When we had all taken our seats, I watched intently as Matthew played his part, eyes closed, moving things around on the board. He called out loudly to the spirits of Elizabeth and Henry, almost begging for them to reveal themselves to the group. Nothing. Then Matthew fixed his gaze straight at me. "Everyone needs to hold hands, or this will not work," he said, unable to conceal his annoyance as he glanced at my right hand. Instead of holding Lily's, as we had been told to, I had rested it just beneath her skirt, touching her thigh. Under the stare of everyone, I removed my hand from its inappropriate location and took Lily's. Matthew began to call upon the spirits once more. This time something did happen; all eight of the lanterns went out simultaneously. The whole group, myself included, gasped, largely due to the sudden darkness that we had been plunged into. There was a nervous laugh as everyone fumbled with their torches. Our hosts did a good job at looking worried, as if they had not been responsible for the lights going out. I shone my torch towards the ceiling, looking for something that would give away the trick, but found nothing.

"That was pretty cool," I admitted to Lily, a little annoyed that I couldn't figure out how it had been done.

"Where's the blonde girl?" I heard someone ask. Turning to my left, I looked down the row of seats to see that Chloe was sat at the far end. The chair next to her now sat empty. The man who had asked the question stood up, looking around, puzzled. He had been sat to her right.

"What do you mean blonde girl?" the goth asked. "I thought you two were together."

"Nope, I came on my own. Looks like she did too."

"Were you not holding her hand?" Matthew asked, looking concerned.

"I was, but she let go as soon as the lights went out."

"Bravo!" I declared. I couldn't help myself laughing at this point. "So, one of the guests disappears, one who happened to come here alone, and who happened to be sitting next to Chloe at the time. You know there's a passageway at that end of the room, right?" The others stood to have a look. I was right, of course, having been in the tunnels before. The passageway entrance was indented into the wall in the far corner and could easily go unnoticed. Everyone seemed to relax, seeing the hoax for what it was. Everyone apart from Matthew and Chloe, who just exchanged worried glances.

"What's her name?" goth girl asked, looking to Chloe. "We should call her back." Chloe looked to Matthew, unsure of how to answer.

"She wasn't with us," Matthew said. "I don't want to cause any panic, but she honestly did come alone, as a paying customer like the rest of you."

"Bullshit," I announced, but I was beginning to doubt my own confidence. The two hosts looked far more worried than anyone else.

"Then maybe she just thought it would be funny," said the guy who had been sat next to her when she disappeared. "I'm sure she'll be back soon."

"I hope so," goth girl said. "But it was you that put out the candles, wasn't it?" she said, looking nervously at Matthew.

"You came for a ghost hunt; don't start to freak out when you actually encounter one." He seemed to have lost his friendliness, however fake it had been, and now appeared on edge, as though he had made a mistake.

"He's got a point." I turned to see Lily standing up, addressing the group. "Whether we honestly thought we would have some kind of paranormal encounter or not, we all came for the frights. We've been to a lot of things like this, and this one doesn't seem much different. Matthew and Chloe are in character and are unlikely to break that unless there is an actual emergency. Whether blondie was an actress, or she thought it would be funny to hide of her own accord, is neither here nor there. The point is, we had a scare, and now we move on to the next part of the tour; isn't that right?" She looked at Matthew, desperately wanting her words to be true.

"Erm," he stuttered, glancing at Chloe, "Yes. That's right. And as someone said, I'm sure the other guest will reappear in due course. Probably quite soon, in fact, as that passageway is where we're heading next." Matthew shone his torch into the narrow entrance, failing to hide his hesitance. "It's a squeeze in here, but this is where the soldiers used to bring the stores of food. There are numerous small storerooms, which come off the passageway. It is also the location of the most frequent sightings of Elizabeth, so keep your eyes peeled."

Four of the group followed behind Matthew, torches flickering to cast as much light as possible in the tight space. I followed, with Lily close behind. I could feel her grabbing on to the back of my jacket. The walls were no more than a foot and a half apart, causing one of the larger guests to turn a little to the side as he walked. No-one spoke, the only sounds being those of heavy breathing and the scraping of clothing along the damp walls as we made our way along. We passed the first two storerooms, one on either side of the passageway. When we reached the entrance to the third, Matthew halted the line.

"If everyone could come into this room please; I have another little story to share with you." We all shuffled in, and it was a relief to see some large electric lights attached to the wall. The brightness was a little dazzling, but certainly made us all feel safer. Everyone turned off their torches, all except Lily, who pointed hers at the floor as if preparing for another blackout.

"Everyone still here?" I asked, glancing around. Eight people; still one less than we started with but no new surprises. Yet. The group murmured as if to confirm their presence and Matthew began to talk, summoning his theatrical voice once again.

"This room is a key part to the story of Henry Oats. It lies directly beneath the location of his home. During our research, we were told by several eyewitnesses, that an image of a bearded man had appeared in this very room on numerous occasions. He did not seem menacing, so please do not be afraid. I will call out to him, and perhaps he will make an appearance." Matthew began calling Henry's name, asking him to make his presence known, but to no avail. The next ten seconds were a blur, however. The electric lamps all went out, again plunging us into darkness, aside from the light from Lily's torch. Everyone made some kind of sound, ranging from a slight gasp to a full-blown scream. Then there was laughter and the room was illuminated again. As I looked toward the sound of the laughter, I saw that it was coming from the man who had been sat next to the blonde lady. He was in hysterics, his hand still resting on the switch for the lighting.

"Fucking arsehole!" the goth girl said.

"I'm sorry; I couldn't resist," the man said, still laughing at his prank. The entire group was looking at him, trying not to give him the satisfaction of actually having terrified all of us. Which is why the whole group saw his face change, from a self-satisfied smirk to pure fear. His eyes widened. His jaw fell slack, as he gazed beyond us. Lily was behind me and as she turned, was the first to let out a scream. Chloe had been stood in the entrance to the room; well, she still was. But now she was merely propped up against the concrete wall. Her eyes bulged, looking as though they would jump from their sockets at any moment. Her skin had turned a paler shade, and her trousers were dark from urine. We all stared for a moment, trying to process the image, trying to persuade ourselves that it was just part of the show. But there was no mistaking that Chloe was dead, the bottom of her torch protruding from her widened mouth, the shaft of it rammed down her throat.

The group parted to allow Matthew through, who tearfully lowered her to the floor. He struggled to pull the torch free, and it came out with the crack of a tooth. He looked stunned, as if he did not know what he was now required to do.

"This is your fault!" he suddenly yelled at the man who'd turned off the lights, before lunging towards him. Matthew shoved him against the wall, before breaking down in tears. It was clear that this was not part of the plan, and most definitely constituted an emergency; everyone pulling out mobile phones to summon help. Of course, so far underground and surrounded by concrete did not bode well for phone reception.

"It must have been that blonde bitch!" someone said.

"Either way, we need to get out of here." No-one disagreed with the goth girl's assessment of the situation and, with torches on, the group piled out of the room and headed back the way that we had come. Lily and I were last to leave the room as I had to do something; get the other key from Chloe. Lily looked away as I rummaged through the dead girl's pockets, eventually locating it and slipping it inside my shoe. I do not know why I did not put it in my pocket but, for some reason, it felt safer being more hidden.

As we moved along to catch up with the others, I heard a clear 'Oh my God!' coming from the front of the line, followed by 'That's impossible!"

"What is it?" I yelled.

"The way we came in. It's blocked."

"What do you mean blocked? With what?" I asked, sure that there was some kind of mistake.

"It's been filled in. Bricked up. There's a fucking wall there now!"

Some of the women in the group had begun to cry at this point, and I could feel the panic rising within us all.

"Turn around!" someone called out. We all did so, putting Lily and myself at the front. I tried to recall what I knew of the tunnels from previous visits, but they looked a little different. Regardless of which way I thought we should go, we really only had the option of continuing along the passageway. We hurried, seven frightened adults squeezing through. *What if this is still only a show, just a really well done one?* I wondered. *Maybe I really underestimated these guys.* It was an optimistic thought, I accepted that, but it did help to keep the panic at bay for a little while longer. Long enough, in fact, for us to reach the end of the passageway. We emerged onto a concrete area with steps going both up and down. I recognized it.

"I know where we are; we can get out up there!" I pointed to the steps and shone my torch. It wasn't far to the top from here, maybe twenty steps at the most. Beyond them, we could make out another iron door, similar to the one we came in through further along the building. I rushed past Lily and up the steps, pushing against the door. It didn't budge. "Matthew!" I called down, into the darkness. "Have you got a key for this?" He came running up to where I was stood.

"I have the key for the door we came in by, try that." He handed me a key which I rammed into the lock. It went in but would not turn.

"It's no good. Shit. Is there another way out?"

"Only the way we came in, if we can find another way around. Or we go down." Matthew did not look happy with this idea. There were seventy-eight steep steps to the bottom, which led to a wide passageway with multiple rooms. The rooms featured several lookout holes in the brick walls which had been used to watch out for the enemy during the war. It was also rumoured to be the most haunted part of the fort.

"We might be able to get someone's attention from down there," I suggested, struggling to stay positive.

"It's getting late; I can't imagine there will be anyone around. But I can't think of anything else to suggest." Matthew looked downtrodden, upset over the death of Chloe, on the verge of giving up himself. Carefully, I made my way back down to the others and explained our options, as far as I could see them, omitting the part about walking straight into the most haunted area here. No-one disagreed, unable to come up with a better plan. Then came the laughter. Not an adult's laughter, but that of a child. It echoed along the concrete walls, ricocheting towards us from where we had just been.

"Elizabeth!" Matthew gasped, his face turning grey. Time seemed to slow at that moment, as every one of us turned our gazes towards the passageway. The laughter became louder, but we saw nothing until that final second. The laughter felt as though it were surrounding us and then silence, just for a second, followed by an unmistakable apparition. A girl, Elizabeth presumably, skin burnt through to muscle and bone, holes where the eyes should have been, stood among us. We watched her mouth slowly open, wider than should be humanly possible, before she released a blood-curdling scream. It startled us all; made us all take a step backward. Unfortunately for the larger man in the group one step back meant a fall down seventy-eight concrete steps. He went with a series of thuds, falling too fast for anyone to try to help him. He must have been half-way down when we heard the crack of bone before he reached the bottom. Elizabeth was gone, all exits were blocked; we had no choice.

The stairway was wide enough for three people to stand side-by-side, so we made our way down in two rows of three, all clinging to one another with six torch beams illuminating our paths. Torchlight soon fell across the body at the bottom of the steps. I felt a little bile rise into my mouth as the cracking sound registered; it must have been his neck breaking. The man's head was looking straight at us, but his body was facing in the opposite direction. Three steps from the bottom, I turned to look back up. The torches were not bright enough to reach the top.

"What's the plan now?" asked the light switch prankster.

"If we head along here, there are some gaps in the wall. We can shout for help and just hope someone hears us."

"And if they don't?"

"Then we really need to get that door open up there or find the one we came in by."

The six of us were huddled together as we walked, torches shining both in front and behind us. We found the first room which branched off of the tunnel; stacks of bricks lay across the floor, covered with blue tarpaulin. There were four or five holes in the wall, maybe ten inches by four. We all fought to see through them, to search for a passer-by. We yelled, we flashed our lights, but had no response.

"Three of us should stay here; the other three can go to the next room. Maybe we'll have more luck that way," Matthew said.

"We should stick together," the goth girl said, shocked by any suggestion of splitting the group up.

"What do you think?" Lily asked me.

"I think the longer we stay down here and the later it gets, the less chance there is of someone happening to pass by. But Matthew is right; it is worth checking out the other room. Don't want to miss the chance if there is someone on that side that we could have not noticed."

"But stick together, or split into two groups?" she asked, as if I was now the leader of this petrified team of reluctant ghost hunters.

"It's just the next room; you, me, and Matthew will check it out, you three keep looking out there and see if anyone comes by. We'll only be a few minutes and if it's no better we'll get back up to that door." The guy who had turned off the lights earlier seemed to see himself as my second-in-command, ordering the goth girl and the other man, who had barely spoken to anyone, to keep watch.

"Keep looking that way please; I'm about to take a piss," he announced as we left the room. The room next door was virtually identical, with the same number of gaps in the brick wall but facing a slightly different angle. We tried, once again, to shout for help, flashing our torches furiously. And once again, it was no use.

"Let's get the others and see what we can do with that door," Lily said. "It's fucking creepy down here."

"As opposed to up there, with the barbecued child?" I said, knowing that staying down here wasn't going to be an option for long.

"She's right," Matthew admitted, looking as though he would cry at any moment. As we exited the room, turning right to grab the others, I walked straight into that loud-mouthed prankster. It startled us both, but he already looked shaken, much more than he had done before needing to relieve himself.

"What?" I asked, dreading the answer.

"You need to look." His face was so full of fear that there was no denying it had to be pretty awful news, more so as he had not seemed all that shaken by the missing woman or the two deaths so far. I almost dropped my torch as I looked into the room that we were in only a few minutes earlier. I had not heard a sound coming from there, nothing to indicate what had happened. Suspended from the ceiling were the goth and the quiet man, hanging by their necks. A sheet of blue tarpaulin used on each of them to hold them in place, draining the life from them.

"What happened?" I asked.

"I don't know," he replied, looking at the ground, the walls, anywhere but at the swinging corpses. "I went for a piss over there." He pointed to a corner of the room where I could make out a wet patch. "They were still looking through those holes; I turned around, and they were...up there." His voice started to break a little, as if trauma was beginning to set in, the reality of our predicament becoming too much.

"We have to go and try the door again," Lily explained once more. "It's our only hope." I held on to her arm tightly and noticed that the two men behind us were now also holding onto each other; fear having replaced any other inhibitions. We hesitated briefly as we passed the broken body at the foot of the steps, before starting our ascent into the darkness. *Seventy-eight*, I reminded myself, counting aloud as we went.

"One, two, three, four..."

"Thirty-seven, thirty-eight, thirty-nine, forty..." Still the torchlight only showed steps ahead.

"Seventy-six, seventy-seven, seventy-eight..." Still more steps. "We should be at the top," I said, stopping for breath. Lily's eyes widened as she shone her light behind us. I turned to see what she had noticed and couldn't process it - there was the body, neck snapped. We were standing on the sixth step up from the bottom.

"Nope," Matthew said, his hands trembling. "Not possible. Just need to keep going." And he started again at the steps, much faster than before, moving ahead of us into the darkness. We walked those steps for what felt like an eternity, losing count as we went. We could hear Matthew panting ahead of us, but always just beyond the torchlights reach.

"I'm at the top!" we heard, not too far ahead of us. Matthew had made it. We kept on until, a few steps further, the whole tunnel was illuminated. Looking up we saw them both, Matthew and Elizabeth, standing at the top of the steps. The light came from the flames which had engulfed

Matthew, and before we could even speak, Elizabeth shoved him towards us. I grabbed Lily towards me, pulling her out of the way of the burning man before he reached her. Our companion was not as fast to react, the fiery, still live, bulk of our tour guide knocking him down into the abyss with a scream. Lily and I looked at each other, silently deliberating whether or not we should follow them, to see if he had survived. Maybe it was the wrong thing to do, but neither of us were brave enough to go back down there, and certainly not when we were this close to the top.

"Elizabeth," Lily called, taking me by surprise.

"What are you doing?" I asked in a whisper.

"I don't know," she replied, sounding desperate. "But I don't want to be set alight and thrown down the bloody steps, so what would you suggest?"

"Elizabeth, are you there?" Lily called out again. Silence for a moment. Then a voice.

"Mummy?" I looked at Lily, having no idea how to respond to that.

"Yes Elizabeth, it's mummy."

"Are you fucking mad?" I hissed.

"Do you know how to open that door up there, Elizabeth?" Lily asked.

"Why do you want the door open?" the voice asked. We took another step upward. There looked like only four or five more, and then the last twenty to the door.

"I thought we could play outside," Lily said, all the while looking at me. "Would you like to play outside?"

"Do you promise not to leave again?" Elizabeth asked.

"Of course. Can I come up? You won't hurt me, will you?"

"I won't hurt you mummy."

"I have a friend with me. Can he come up as well?" *Great,* I thought. *What if she says no?*

"Only if he is nice," was the response.

"He is very nice; I promise. Now, can you open the door for us?" There was a pause, followed by a creaking sound. Light poured in from the now-open door, light which emanated from the streetlights on the fort's concourse. We ran toward the door, knowing that it was our only chance. I practically dragged Lily out into the cold air, running as fast as I could towards the locked gates. As we neared them, we heard banging coming from the door we had used to enter the tunnels, a muffled voice behind it, asking for help. *Blondie!* As I searched in my shoe for the key to the padlock, Lily yanked at the iron doors. They were not locked but were stiff with age. Lily found some wood nearby, thin enough to wedge between the door and frame, providing sufficient leverage to prise it open. As the blonde fell out into the open, Elizabeth's burnt figure appeared again. What was left of her face was distorted in anger.

"Where is my mummy?" she screamed. I clicked open the padlock, yanking the chain away from the gates. I had to make a decision, and I'm not proud of it.

"Elizabeth, she's here," I shouted. The girl's eyeless stare turned to me. "Get ready to run," I told Lily, quietly. Grabbing the blonde girl, I shoved her towards Elizabeth, with a whisper of 'sorry'.

"Mummy!" the girl cried, disappearing back through the door with the woman whom I had just sacrificed. Lily looked distraught, almost disgusted by my actions, but did not pause for long. We shoved open the gates and ran, full pelt, all the way back to our house. Once we were safely inside, with every lock in place and every light turned on, we sat to get our story straight. It had to be reported, we knew that, but we also knew how crazy it would sound.

An hour after we had called the police, they arrived at our house. They threatened us with wasting police time. They had searched the whole place and there was no sign of foul play; no bodies, no Ouija board, nothing out of place. They told us that they had called the events manager of the fort and been told that nothing had been booked in for that evening - there had been no ghost hunt. The more we insisted that we were telling the truth, the more we were told we would be arrested for wasting their resources. Lily and I were stuck with the memories of that night, unable to explain them, unable to share them with anyone else. And that has been our curse ever since.

Collection III:
The Artist & Other Stories

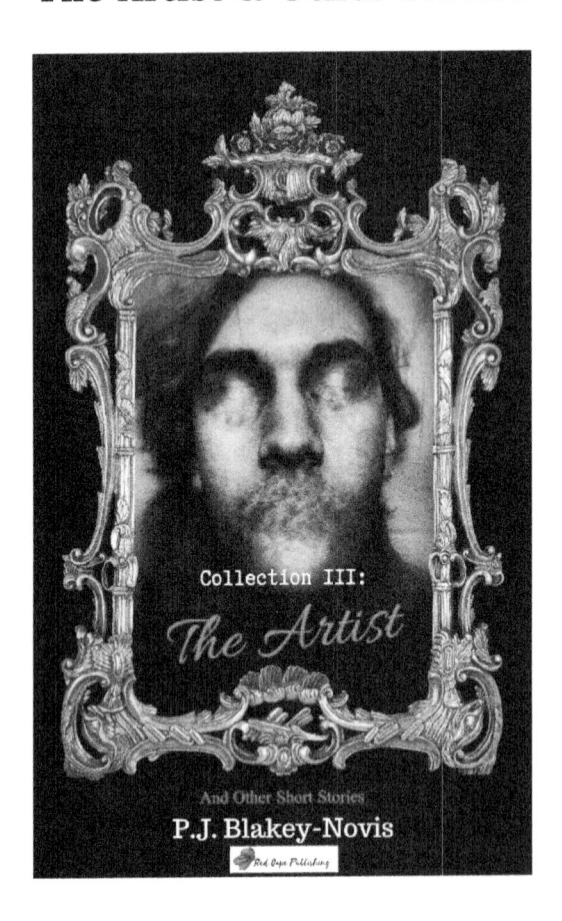

THE ARTIST

Everyone told me that I was gifted from a young age. I must have been about four or five when I first picked up a set of pencils and began to sketch. Straight lines were easy, so I drew incredibly detailed pictures of my bedroom to begin with. Each piece of furniture was meticulously brought to life. I spent days on each image. I'd take the drawings into school to show off to my teachers, who rewarded me with compliments and stickers.

It wasn't until I began secondary school, when Art became its own lesson, that my talent began to be talked about with more excitement. The Art faculty at my school was small, made up of only two teachers. In my first year of secondary school I was taught by Mr. Low, a man in his late sixties who was happy to have his students painting pictures of fruit, or simple landscapes. He gave the impression, which may well have been very accurate, that he did not expect much from his students. Perhaps this was why I stood out. While my classmates were happy to soak the paper in paint, lines of green for the grass, blue for the sky, and a yellow splodge for the sun, I would create pieces that were almost photographic in their quality.

Mr. Low said I was an A-grade student, a talented kid. Nevertheless, he explained that I needed to focus on more useful subjects, or else I'd end up as an Art teacher. To me, that sounded like a great career choice, but the disappointment in his voice suggested otherwise. Drawing and painting were what I loved, and I was determined to make a future out of it. I could never have imagined just what form that would take, or the damage my choices would do.

"How do you make a living as an artist?" I asked him, at the end of one lesson when my classmates had left the room. He looked at me sadly.

"Create a lot of works. And be dead. The big money only really comes posthumously. Or learn to paint portraits. There is a market for portraits still, and it's only the wealthy that could buy them."

The first school year went by quickly, with all my spare time sketching in the book I carried on me at all times. I took books from the library which claimed to teach one how to draw people. Too shy to ask anyone to sit for me, I copied people from magazines, film posters, even pausing the television and drawing the news reporters. As with most things in life, the more I practiced, the better I became.

A week before the start of the summer break, I decided to sketch Mr. Low, from his photograph on the school's website. It turned out well, my best so far, and I knew that he would be pleased with it. Even his profile photo looked sad. I didn't know much about him, not really. He wore a wedding ring but had never talked about his life outside of school. *I wish you could have made it as an artist,* I thought as I looked at my portrait. I scribbled a signature at the bottom before rolling it up and securing it with an elastic band. I was right that Mr. Low would like the picture; he seemed genuinely impressed with it.

"Where do you think you will put it?" I asked, eagerly.

"I have a little studio in my garage, where I paint. It can go in there."

"I'd like to see your paintings some time," I replied with sincerity.

"You can," he said. "There are a few seascapes in the pub near the beach. They've been there a few years now, not that anyone has ever bought any."

"Sir," I began. "I'm twelve. I don't tend to go to the pub." Mr. Low looked at me a little puzzled.

"Of course, yes. Well, maybe your parents can take you in to see the paintings one day."

It was a couple of weeks into the summer break when we first headed to the beach. My dad was working most days, so it was just my mum, Jenny (my little sister), and myself. The beach is only a twenty-minute walk from our house and would have been lazy to drive there, mum said. Of course, at my age I was unfamiliar with the pubs and hadn't thought much more about what Mr. Low had told me. Now I saw it, though. As we turned the last corner approaching the beach, there was the pub that he had mentioned to me.

"Can we go in the pub?" I asked. Mum looked at me a little surprised. We didn't go to pubs; it just wasn't the sort of place that our parents took us.

"Why on earth do you want to go to the pub?"

"My art teacher has some paintings in there. He said to have a look if I could."

"They have a tree house with a slide around the back," Jenny piped up. Mum looked bewildered.

"Now, how do you know that?" she asked.

"Rachel's mum took us here last week, when I went around to play."

"Did she now?" Mum mumbled. "OK, I'll tell you what. Let's get an orange juice each and sit out the back for a little bit. You can see the paintings and have a little play. Then we get to the beach before the tide starts coming back in."

"Can I have wine?" Jenny asked.

"No, you're eight. Ten more years." With that, we made our way inside. Mum ordered three orange juices, before asking how to get out to the garden. I scanned the walls, finding no paintings. There were rectangular marks on the paintwork, as though the sunlight had not reached them, as if something had been hung there until recently. I pulled at mum's sleeve.

"I can't see the paintings." Mum glanced around. "Can you ask someone?"

"Excuse me," she said, looking at the barmaid who had served our drinks. "My son's art teacher told him he had some paintings here on display?"

"All gone, I'm afraid. Someone bought them all."

"Well, there you go," Mum told me.

"That can't be right. He said he hasn't sold any for years!" The barmaid looked at me.

"They were here for quite a while. Probably a tourist coming through with money to burn."

When the time came to return to school, I couldn't wait to talk to Mr. Low. I knew he'd be happy that he had sold the paintings, but he wasn't there. All the school office would tell me was that he had resigned. I didn't know where he lived, or how to contact him, and I could have cried. It was three days before we had our first art lesson, and I was anxious about who would be taking the class.

"My name is Miss Starlight," she announced as we took to our seats. We all knew her name, as she had been the other half of the art faculty, but no-one actually believed that Starlight was her real name. Most of the male students referred to her as the 'hot hippie', whilst the female students complained about the injustice of not being allowed to dye their hair whilst the art teacher sported bright blue dreadlocks. "As some of you may know, Mr. Low is no longer working here. I will be taking your art lessons until a replacement is found."

"Why did he leave?" I blurted out, uncharacteristically talking in front of the class.

"You sad 'cos your boyfriend left?" Matthew said, causing a wave of laughter. My fondness for Mr. Low had been the subject of mockery before, and I had done my best to ignore it, but Matthew was an unpleasant individual.

"Actually, he had a rather good reason. An art dealer approached him and has purchased all of his paintings, with the intention of buying more. He has decided to focus on this, instead of teaching. Anyway, on with the lesson. For the next few weeks we are going to focus on expressionism, and you are to draw, paint, or sculpt, a piece which represents one of your classmates. I'll be choosing who is paired with whom. Now, the piece of work can be anything you like; you may draw something as lifelike as possible, or shapes and colours that the person brings to mind. It really is down to you."

"Can I be paired with Claire?" Matthew asked. Everyone looked at him, confused by the request. Claire was even less popular than me; obese, with glasses and ginger hair - the easiest of victims for a bully. "That way, I can just draw a ginger blob, and it will be spot-on." There was laughter again, but not from me. I fixed Matthew with a glare, my anger at his cruelty overpowering my usual cowardice. Claire began to sob, which only added to the laughter from Matthew and his group.

"That's a detention for you," Miss Starlight said, trying to conceal her own contempt for the boy. "No-one will want to work with you if you treat people like that." Miss Starlight pulled a brown envelope out from her desk drawer. "In here I have everyone's names. I'll pull out two at a time, and those people will be working together for this project. It's not optional, so I suggest you all make the best of it. And if anyone creates something that I deem to be malicious, there will be consequences."

I didn't honestly care who I got put with; I could draw anyone so would just do it as accurately as possible. Even so, it was pretty rotten luck that I got paired with Matthew. My first instinct was to draw a very detailed dick picture, deep purple veins, a bulbous head spewing out semen which looked like speech bubbles from a comic. I could then fill in text with all the nasty stuff he said on a daily basis. I grinned without realising I was doing so.

"Something funny?" Matthew asked.

"Nope," I lied. I knew I wouldn't actually draw what I wanted to, but it made me feel better to know I *could*, if I was just a little braver. Instead, I concentrated on drawing Matthew as skilfully as I could, all the while dreading what he would come up with. The class seemed, much to Miss Starlight's surprise, to take to the task quite well. The room was quiet; only the sounds of pencils and brushes against paper could be heard. By the time the bell rang to signify the end of class, I had made good progress with the outline of Matthew's face.

"How's yours going?" I asked him.

"You'll see when it's finished." He gave me a smile that made me nervous. Looking back, it was probably a mistake on Miss Starlight's part to finish the project by getting each of us to stand before the class and hold up our work, certainly without her checking the pieces first. When the time came, at the end of the third lesson on this project, we were called up to show what we had done. I suppose that mine was as expected; very good as sketches go, clearly a picture of who I was assigned to draw. Black and white pencil shading, on a sheet of A3 sized paper. Matthew shuffled a few sheets of A4 as he stood up, winking at me.

"I'm not very good at drawing, Miss," he explained. "So, I came up with something that I think represents the subject well." I felt my stomach turn as I watched him apply sticky tape to the sheets, fixing them against the whiteboard. "It's like a comic, Miss. So, you may have to come closer to see it properly." Matthew's mates jumped up first, knowing that they needed to get a look before the teacher did. Their howls of laughter told me that I didn't want to see, but I couldn't help myself, and just made it before Miss Starlight ripped them down. It was nothing but a series of stickman drawings, the first featuring (presumably) me giving a picture to a taller stickman with grey hair (presumably Mr. Low). This was followed by the pair of us in various positions, I didn't catch them all, but in one Mr. Low had me bent over his desk as I said 'thank-you'. I wasn't surprised by Matthew's 'work', but I knew it would something that was talked about for a long time; teenagers could be an unforgiving bunch.

Of course, Matthew would be punished, and the pictures destroyed, but that wouldn't make much difference. I tried not to react, but I felt my face redden, and became desperate not to cry. I felt powerless, and this is perhaps the worst feeling in the world. Miss Starlight kept me behind after class that day, wanting to check that I was alright. I pretended that I was, and there was little more that she could have done.

"For what it's worth," she began, "you'll be getting a good mark for the drawing. It really is excellent." I looked at it, anger burning in my eyes.

"I wish he would go away," I told Miss Starlight. "If only he would break a leg or something, anything to keep him away from here for a while." The teacher stayed silent for a moment.

"Are you OK walking home? I don't want any trouble outside of school if Matthew is still about." I hadn't thought about this, but I rarely saw them outside of school as we lived in opposite direction, so I said I'd be fine and made my way out across the car park. There are two exits from the school, and I take the one to the left which leads on to the new-build housing estate that I live on. But something pulled me in the other direction that day, a sound of commotion, the flickering of blue lights reflected in the windows of parked cars, so I made my way towards the growing group of teenagers and passers-by. At the back of the crowd I spotted Claire and asked her what was going on. She grinned at me.

"Matthew got run over!" she whispered, a little too excitedly. "He's not dead or anything, but his leg looks pretty mashed up. It snapped the wrong way at the knee." I felt sick; I knew my face had gone pale, and my legs felt odd. I didn't reply to Claire, just turned and headed towards home. *If only he would break a leg or something.* My words came back to haunt me. *Coincidence!* I told myself. I couldn't stop thinking about it for the rest of the day, all the way up to falling asleep. At three in the morning I woke up, suddenly, and was hot by another thought. *I wish you could have made it as an artist.* I couldn't get back to sleep after that, my logical brain telling me that I was being stupid.

Climbing out of bed and switching on the lamp on my desk, I grabbed a pencil and paper. I looked around for inspiration, my eyes falling on a photograph of Jenny taken at a dance show. Quickly, I began sketching her; it wasn't my best work, but the resemblance was obvious.

"Wake up, and come to my room," I said to the picture, feeling more than a little silly. I sat in my chair, holding my breath, listening out for signs of movement. And then it came; little footsteps down the hallway, my bedroom door creaking open. My heart raced, wanting to believe this was a coincidence but knowing it could not be. Jenny stood there holding her stuffed rabbit, rubbing at her eyes.

"What's up?" I asked. She looked around, clearly confused.

"Nothing. Sorry, I don't know. Must have been dreaming." I sent her back to bed, my mind reeling. The possibilities were endless, if not a little terrifying, but there had to be some limitations to this supposed power; I just had no way to fully grasp it. I drew mum, told the picture that she should give me £10 in the morning to buy sweets with. If this worked, then there was no way that it was coincidence. Mum never bought sweets, and she never gave us money for ourselves.

At 7.30am I was on my way to school, a crisp ten-pound note in my pocket, and a list of ways I could improve the world swirling around in my mind. I felt a little guilt over Matthew's accident, but only a little, and at that time I never considered using this power to hurt people. I still don't know how I reached this point.

Over the rest of my school years, I felt invincible. I drew Claire next, telling her to exercise regularly and eat better. And she did; by the following school year she was of an average size, and her confidence had much improved. She even got a boyfriend, albeit a nerdy guy with greasy hair and horrific acne. I drew bullies, and they soon had minor accidents. Nothing like the broken leg Matthew suffered, which took almost six months to heal, but little things like tripping over in front of people or urinating themselves during school plays. I fantasised about winning the lottery as I turned old enough to buy a ticket but couldn't figure out a way to make that happen, so resorted to telling people to give me things. It started with my parents, of course, from that time I told my mum to give me ten pounds for sweets, but I started to feel what I assume was guilt. A while after this, I started drawing some of the kids I didn't like and told them to bring me money. By the time I was seventeen, I had ten kids at school each giving me £20 each on a daily basis. I didn't know where they were getting it, and I didn't care. I was getting greedy.

At eighteen, and still a virgin, I used my power to get laid. I'm not proud of it, but I did it. It also wasn't all that good, but I had the pick of the school and despite all being over much quicker than I had hoped, I did get to see a beautiful girl naked. I felt guilty afterward, more so than I had over any of my other actions, as though I had forced it to happen. I suppose I did, in fact. I vowed to never do it again, but hormones, and my lack of any genuine offers, meant that I could not be trusted in this way. Soon I had slept with a number of young women, all of whom believed it had been their idea, so no one was really hurt by my actions.

Until Madison. The girls before her had been conquests; a display of my new-found power, and the fulfilment of my urges. Madison was different, and we were together a number of times. I was getting better at doing the deed, and I started to fall for her. I told the drawing of her to come and find me for sex, and she would. I told the drawing to love me, for her to be with me, and she did. We were perfect together, although no-one could understand what she saw in me, including herself. I left all the drawings alone, apart from hers, and for a year we spent all our time with each other.

I had several drawings of her, in varying states of undress, stuck to my bedroom wall. I would talk to them, tell them what I wanted. Aside from the sexual side of the relationship, I simply told her to love me, to stay with me for all time. My exact words were 'until death do us part'. I thought it was a reasonably request; I knew I could be good to her and although it may have been somewhat false, she would have believed herself to be happy with me. I was naive. I thought love was possible at such a young age, but it was merely an illusion. I could control people's actions, that much was clear. But perhaps it was too much to control how they honestly felt? Maybe it only worked when we were together?

After our first year together I heard a rumour about another guy that Madison had been seeing. I didn't believe it; I couldn't see how it would be possible if she loved me. So, I asked her outright, and she began to cry.

"I'm sorry," she told me. "This thing between us is weird, and I can't take it anymore. You know, I don't even think about you when I'm not here. I just suddenly get the urge to see you; it's as if it's out of my hands. I can't explain it. I told my friend, and she said you've hypnotized me or something. That I wouldn't go for you out of choice."

"You have to stay with me," I said, almost pleading.

"Look at me, not those fucking drawings, when you say that!" she said. "You can't make me stay." Madison turned to leave, intending to walk out of my life forever, but I couldn't let that happen.

"Sit down!" I said, commanding the pencil drawing of her face. Madison sat, a little surprised at her own actions. Something in me changed in that moment, a desire to show off how powerful I was, a need for revenge against my love that had forsaken me. "I can make you do anything I please," I told her. She looked afraid but did not try to move. "Watch."

"Take off your top," I told the picture. Madison began to undress, but it was clear that she did not want to; her hands were obeying me, but her mind was trying to fight it. "See?" I asked. She did not reply, just stared at me through widened eyes, struggling to process what was happening.

"I told you that you were to stay with me, until death did us part. That's not something we can change. But I don't know if I can forgive you for betraying me. Are you even sorry?"

"Not at all," she said, defiantly. "You're fucking crazy!" I didn't mean to say what came next.

"Then we're finished. And you are so upset that you can't go on living any longer. Now get out!" Madison looked at me as if I were insane, hastily putting her top back on, before walking out and slamming the door behind her. I broke down in tears at the loss of my love, and over what I knew was now inevitable.

News broke the next day of Madison's suicide, a bathtub filled with crimson water, deep slices down each of her forearms. The note she left blamed me, and rightly so, but everyone assumed it was because I had ended our relationship. I had gone too far, and although I had no intention in following in Madison's footsteps, I knew that I needed to get this power under control. I thought back over the last few years and the wasted opportunity to use my talent for the good of others. Greed and lust had been my downfall and had ended in death. I knew I could never draw again, but doubted I had the willpower to resist.

I considered breaking my fingers, or pounding my hands with a hammer, but feared they would heal in time. There was only one way to be certain that I never drew again, one way to make sure I could not look at another picture and control that person. I searched through the draw of my desk until I came across my fountain pen; an unused gift from my dad for my eighteenth birthday. I took a deep breath before plunging it as quickly as I could into my right eye, the pain far more excruciating than I had expected. *Don't stop,* I told myself, ramming it into my left eye and twisting, causing a wet sensation to run down my face. I tried to look around but could see nothing; it worked. Finally, everyone was safe.

THE CHILDREN OF THE DEEP

I could begin to tell this story by suggesting I enjoyed going for long walks at night. That, perhaps, would be a strange activity to take part in. The truth is that I would regularly walk home from a drinking session, having missed the last bus, busy with those final few shots. There were pubs nearer to my home than the one I chose to frequent, but they were either less pleasant venues, or had priced me out. As a result, I made The Traveller's Rest my regular hide-out; a traditional British pub in which every surface was sticky, and one could still detect the odour of stale tobacco smoke, despite smoking in pubs having been banned back in 2006. However, to its merit, The Traveller's drinks were priced in a way more suited to my budget, and the pub featured a beer garden which overlooked the English Channel. In fact, due to the erosion of the local coastline, the pub was now positioned a little too close to the cliff edge for comfort, and staff were known to escort especially inebriated customers out to taxis to ensure they didn't wander the wrong way and end up mashed on the rocks below.

June 1st was a typical Friday evening for me, aside from the air temperature being a good ten degrees warmer than usual. Perhaps this was to be the start of the fabled British summer; heat we are unaccustomed to, complain about, then miss terribly when it disappears a fortnight later. On this particular Friday I had finished work in the nearest city, where I had been cooped up in a call-centre all day trying (unsuccessfully) to sell life insurance and alighted the bus outside The Traveller's Rest. It was on the route which took me home, which was convenient, but the walk back afterwards would be a good forty minutes, or more, depending on how much I drank. And I drank a lot.

This evening played out the same as so many before; I arrived at the bar around 6pm, I ordered two pints of strong scrumpy and two double whiskeys and made my way out to the garden. I always ordered two of each drink, as the first one would go down too quickly, and I hated having to queue at the bar. Thankfully, my usual table was clear. I headed there out of habit now, having soon learned that it was the only outside table which didn't wobble if you leaned on it. I gazed out across the stillness of the Channel, knocking back the drinks, and making my way through almost an entire twenty-pack of Superkings. I lost track of time as I made my way back from the bar to my table with my twelfth pint of scrumpy and had just sat (rather heavily) back down when I heard the bell ring for 'time at the bar'. I knew I had maybe ten to fifteen minutes to finish my drink, before one of the bar staff would remind me that I needed to go home. I also knew that the last bus home had left almost half an hour ago.

It may have been the heat, which didn't mix well with such quantities of alcohol, but I felt exhausted. Drunkenly, I checked my wallet, dropping it in the process, but it contained no notes. I could feel a pile of loose coins in my right pocket, but upon inspection it did not appear to be enough to pay for a cab. I would have to walk again, and this time I didn't think I'd make it. The idea of sleeping out on the grass, a little way along from the pub, crossed my mind, but I was too terrified of rolling over the cliff edge in my sleep. So, I started walking.

Now, there are two fairly direct routes from the Traveller's to my home. The safest, and the one I always take, is to simply follow the main road for a couple of miles and take just one turning off it. At a sober walking pace, it is around a thirty-minute walk, but in my usual evening condition, it can be anything from forty to fifty minutes. There is also a short cut, but as with any short cuts, it comes with a degree of risk. A pretty significant risk, actually, even if one were sober when attempting it.

There is an area of coastline between my current location and my home, which would be described as treacherous. It is essentially a quarter mile of rocks and boulders, interspersed with rock pools, rusty shopping trolleys, and even a very old car which came over the cliff in the 1950s. However, it isn't merely the terrain which makes for difficult travelling. This stretch of coastline is on a curve, meaning that you simply cannot see around to the safety of the next beach until you are almost upon it. In fact, it is more like two curves, a soft 'w' shape, if you like. I remember reading the coast guards warning before, which explained that, even if you time it right, you only have about thirty minutes to traverse the rocks before the tide cuts you off. Although there are a multitude of warning signs suggesting that it would be unwise to attempt it, thirty minutes is plenty of time to make it across. At least, it's plenty of time if the tide is fully out, and you are sober and agile. On this evening, I was none of those things, and the tide, despite appearing to be out, was actually returning, in what seemed to be a hurry.

Now of course, choosing to take this short cut was a stupid idea, but stupid ideas seem to come to me often when I'm drunk, and drunk is something that I usually am. Having convinced myself the tide was far enough out, that I wouldn't have any issues with climbing across boulders in my work shoes (when walking in a straight line was more than a little challenging), and that this was a much quicker route home, I began the descent on to the rocks. I just hope that I wouldn't have attempted it if the moon wasn't providing such superb luminescence, but with the help of my mobile phone's flashlight app, I could see well enough. I didn't get half-way.

The tide had made its way back in, splashing gently against the cliff face in the central part of the soft 'w'. I wasn't happy, and considered swimming, before my brain reminded me that I'd certainly drown. Annoyed at having wasted more time trying to get home, I turned back, hurrying myself over a particularly large boulder, and looked ahead for the entry point. I could see the metal bars which signified the end of the promenade, the moonlight glinting off the metal. Then panic gripped me. Between the promenade, and my position on the rocks, was nothing but seawater. The warnings from all those signs that I had chosen to ignore came to mind, and I began to tremble. I climbed on to a higher rock, looking behind me to see that the tide had risen another metre or so in the last few minutes. I had two choices; try to swim for it or call the coastguard. Even in the state I was in, swimming felt like a stupid idea, beyond even my own levels of foolishness. There was no telling how deep the water was, how strong the current would be, and there were all manner of threatening rocks beneath the surface which could do me damage. It would have to be a call to the coast guard, and a prayer that they arrived quickly. I fumbled with my phone, the flashlight pointing at my now green and slimy shoes. I pressed the '9' button three times. The operative answered, and I turned. I have a habit of pacing when on the telephone, and my brain had not warned my feet that now was not the time. I took a step, and before I could explain my predicament, my foot slipped from the side of the rock, and everything went black.

My phone was long-gone when I came to, so I couldn't have told you how long I had been out, even if the thought had entered my head at the time. What I do remember was the music, soft and rhythmic, as though being played on a harp, or perhaps a lyre. The tune was unfamiliar, and I must have been listening to its soothing melody for a few minutes before I even tried to open my eyes. There was another sound in the background, water lapping against stone. That's when it all flooded back to me; the drinks, the rock climbing, the getting cut off by the tide. But where was I? I'd clearly been knocked out from the fall, so I should have drowned. Unless the coastguard found me in time? I had a vague recollection of calling them, but did I even tell them where I was? The memory was too hazy to be certain.

I opened my eyes, half-expecting to be in a hospital, and the sounds to be my imagination, but I was not. It was dark, but not the wild darkness of night-time. There was no mistaking that I was in a cave, but the walls glowed with a turquoise hue, reminding me of an episode of Blue Planet which talks about the phosphorescent creatures in the deep ocean. I looked to my left and right, seeing nothing but natural illumination on the cave walls which appeared to stretch as far as I could see in both directions. I closed my eyes, trying to focus my hearing. The music, if that is what it was, came from my right. The sound of water was not coming from my left or right and was unmistakably coming from *above* me.

The music, eerie as it was, seemed to call to me. I tried to stand, fumbling in the darkness, my hands pressing against the slimy walls for support. It was damp, but not cold, and I ran my hands down my now crumpled shirt and across my rear to discover that I was completely dry. This struck me as odd, but I couldn't quite establish why. I had to choose a direction and had no clue which way to go; the only noticeable thing was the music. However, music meant people surely, so it made sense to follow the sound. In the poor lighting, I continued to trip over rocks, splash in shallow pools, and run my hands over unpleasant feeling surfaces as I made my way. There was no way of telling how far, or for how long, I had travelled, but it felt as though hours had passed.

The music remained as clear as it had been when I first came around, but no louder. I wondered if my mind was playing tricks on me, or whether I had simply not made it far enough. I looked back for the first time, considering whether I should have gone the other way, but it appeared different. Darker than I remembered. Shadows seemed to move against the walls of what now was unmistakably a lengthy network of tunnels. I shivered, not through cold, but a hint of fear gripped me. Of course, I was already afraid; being lost and potentially trapped, in the dark is rather terrifying, but this was something different, something sinister.

Heading back felt dangerous, so I kept going, speeding up as well as I could on such terrain. I refused to turn around, certain that I could detect shadows moving in the far-reaches of my eyesight. Just when I thought that the tunnel had no end, the distance between the walls began to widen, weakening the reach of the phosphorescent light, and forcing me to choose a side. The music appeared to come from both directions, so I kept to the right, without much thought, as my hand continued to slide across the surface. Following the wall as it sloped further away from its counterpart, the music finally grew louder. I paused, the beating of my heart audible above the stringed instrument, and chanced a look around. I could make out the light from the wall I had left behind, snaking its way in a circular formation, finishing at the point at which I stood. I may have awoken in a tunnel, but I was most certainly in a cave now. I could just about make out the entrance to the cave which I had passed through, and a different kind of light near to it. I stared, trying to focus my eyes, certain that I had not missed a red light on my way through.

It was small, and I wondered if it was the light from a phone, or other electronic device. I strained my eyes, debating whether or not to head towards it, when I realised there was more than one red light. Six, in fact. And moving in pairs. Not just moving, but moving in my direction, shrouded in jet black shadow. I had to run, my fight or flight reflex told me as much, but the practicality of gaining any speed in a dark and treacherous cave meant I was unsuccessful. I felt cold as they approached, my hairs standing on end, my pupils dilating as I saw my demise approach. And then nothing.

There did not appear to be any time between that encounter and me suddenly standing on a candle lit, circular stone floor. It was as if I had simply been transported from one location to another, but I suppose I had been heading in this direction anyway. I studied my surroundings, trying to understand my situation a little better, but to no avail. I was still in the cave, but the turquoise light I had followed so faithfully now appeared perhaps forty or fifty feet above me. I was stood on a circle of stone, some thirty feet in diameter, but it was not a natural feature of the location. The stone was carved with intricate designs, none of which were familiar to me, although something about them made me uneasy. I wouldn't have known with any certainty if they were occult symbols, but this was the first thought that came to mind. In the very centre of the stone circle stood a robed figure, playing on an ancient version of a harp. I could not make out their appearance as the robe ran from head to foot, the hood largely obscuring their face. Even so, it was evident from the hands alone that the musician was female, with young-looking skin.

I glanced around once more, nervous about the return of those shadows, but saw none. I continued to stand there, not wanting to interrupt the music; something about the situation made me certain that I should wait to be spoken to. When she showed no sign of stopping playing, I had no choice but to speak.

"Where am I?" I asked. The music stopped abruptly.

"You are here," came the soft voice.

"Where is here?" I replied, a little irritated by the stupid answer I had been given.

"Home," she said.

"Your home?" I wondered, doubtful that anyone could actually live in a cave, no matter how mad they were.

"Our home."

"Enough of the cryptic bullshit," I told her, my angry words seeming much louder than I had intended as they echoed from the damp walls of the cave. I thought I detected a sigh leave her mouth. Slowly, she placed the instrument on the ground and lifted the hood from her head. I was taken aback by how beautiful she was. She then proceeded to remove the fastenings beneath her chin, slipping the robe from her shoulders and allowing it to drop to the floor. I struggled to keep my mouth closed as I took in her full nudity.

"Erm, what's going on?" I asked, a little bashfully. "Who are you?" She took a step towards me.

"I'm The Mother," she said, her green eyes twinkling with something mischievous. Her red lips parted a little as she cocked her head to the side, almost playfully.

"Whose mother?" I was unsure if I wanted to know the answer to this. She ignored the question.

"My children saved you." I tried to remember what had happened but could recall nothing after slipping from the boulder I had been standing on.

"And where are your children now?" I asked nervously, trying to politely look at her face when speaking to her.

"They are around, playing somewhere, no doubt."

"I need to get home," I told her. As nice as it was to speak to a beautiful, naked woman (something I had not had the pleasure of for some time), the situation was too bizarre and unless it was all a dream, I knew it couldn't end well.

"Up top?" she asked, a glint of anger flashing across her face. I didn't understand at first, but quickly realised that we had to be beneath ground level.

"Yes, how do I get back there? I don't remember how I came into this place." She appeared to be thinking about my question.

"My children can take you back, if that's what you really want?" I looked at her, unsure of how to word my next statement.

"Well, I can't very well just disappear and live in this cave with you!" I stated, as if it were the most obvious thing in the world, which I suppose it was. She looked displeased with my words.

"Very well. Just know that they will only take you back to where they found you. The tide is high, and you will be returned to that very place. I just hope you are an exceptionally strong swimmer. Children!" The woman shouted for her children, smiling as three pairs of red eyes seemed to float towards me, impossibly black shadows surrounding them. I stepped back, afraid of what they would do. "If you change your mind," she said, her smile returning, "just call out for me. However, if you do come back, I would have to insist that you stay."

Before I could answer, I was gone from that room, suddenly ice-cold, and unable to breathe. As promised, I had been returned to the exact spot that I had landed from my fall, now a good four metres below sea level. The tide pulled me back and forth, far stronger than I could fight against. The saltwater burned my eyes, so I scrunched them shut and tried to swim in the direction I believed to be up. I did not have the strength, and pure terror overwhelmed me. My chest felt as if it would explode as I tried to hold my breath. Eventually, I could hold it no longer and took in a lungful of seawater.

It is a natural impulse to want to survive, and I wasn't in a position to weigh up my options. I knew I was close to death and, clinging to some illogical hope that it would work, I called out. She had only referred to herself as The Mother so that was the word I used. With a lungful of water, and on the verge of unconsciousness, I could make no sound, but my thought was heard somewhere in that underground room. A fraction of a second later I was spluttering up seawater across the stone circle that I found myself lying upon.

"I'm glad you returned," she said with a smile.

"I didn't have a lot of choice," I retorted. "And I don't intend to stay."

"I made your options clear to you," she warned. "Now you are wet through. Put this on." She handed me a gown, identical to her own, which she must have fetched knowing that I would return in this state. Reluctantly, I removed my clothes and slipped it on. She looked at me approvingly. "Now you are ready." She turned on her heel, walking to the far side of the circle. Standing above a carving of what looked like a doorway, with horned creatures around it, she closed her eyes and mumbled something indiscernible. I watched in surprise as the ground opened to reveal crude steps descending further into the earth. I followed, certain I had no option, and knowing there was no way out from where I stood.

Flaming torches adorned the walls of a narrow tunnel, and I kept a few paces behind, still shivering from the cold water, trying to avert my gaze from her naked rear. The tunnel began to twist and turn, heading off in different directions, until I had no idea which way would lead back. And then we were at, what I assumed, was our destination. It took me a few moments to understand what was happening; the candles were no surprise, but there were at least twenty other people sitting in the room, all of whom looked too old to still be breathing. I noticed that they all wore the same black robes except one; a single, red-robed person was seated at the front. They sat in rows, with a walkway between them, facing the far end of the cavern. At the end of the walkway was an altar of some kind, an undoubtedly satanic image etched into the sandstone above.

My first thought was that I would become a sacrifice; that some devil worshipping cult would cut me to pieces and bathe in my blood. No one looked around as we entered, and she whispered to me to remove my robe. I didn't want to, but was significantly outnumbered if this went badly, whatever this was. She took my hand, and we walked towards the alter, naked as the day we were born. As we stood before it, the red robe approached us, a decorative cushion in her hands. The hands were old, wrinkled and twisted with arthritis. On the cushion sat two rings, and the gravity of the situation hit me just as hard as the icy water had done not long ago. I was about to be married. We stood, in traditional wedding fashion, facing one another. She leaned in and whispered in my ear.

"You have to go along with it, or they will kill you." I nodded, not doubting that she was telling the truth.

"But why me?" I asked, before the ceremony could begin.

"You were available. We saved you, and now you need to save us." I had no time to ask any more questions, as the red-robed official began mumbling in an unknown language. I looked around the crowd to see everyone staring at us in silence. But the thing that struck me was that all the spectators were female; not a man in sight. It all felt too solemn for me to interrupt, as crazy as that sounds. I couldn't take in what was happening, and stood in silence, as though I were numb. Before I knew it, rings were placed on our fingers, and we were ushered through a small doorway into a tiny room containing only a bed.

"I need to know what the hell is going on," I said, once we were alone. I tried to keep my tone forceful, but not angry. My words came out feeble and frightened.

"I am The Mother, the chosen one. Until my children grow, I am the youngest, and the only fertile member of our kind."

"Your kind?" I repeated. The suggestion that these were not human sounded ridiculous at first, but I had been transported from one location to another in the blink of an eye, and those shadow creatures were certainly not of this world.

"We have survived for centuries, finding mates as and when our numbers dwindled. We have gone by many names over the years before now. Sailors called us sirens, telling tales of how our singing would cause them to crash their ships. This was never the case; we helped people who were in danger. We just asked for something in return."

"A husband? That's insane." Again, her eyes registered something akin to anger.

"Usually just a mate, to continue our line. I wanted more."

"So, what? We are supposed to live happily ever after in a cave full of old women, and just make babies?" As soon as I'd said it, it didn't sound quite as bad as I'd thought. "And what were those shadow things? You called them your children, but they were something else."

"Just lie down." My brain told me that I didn't want to, but other parts of my body suggested otherwise. She touched me, gently guiding me onto the bed. I told myself to just go with it, and then work out how to escape after, still clinging to the hope that this was simply a dream. As she had her way with me, not entirely against my will, she began mumbling in the same old language I had heard before. Her breath quickened, her face became flushed with red. I could feel myself reaching the end and, with her weight on top of me, knew there was no way to stop this happening. As I climaxed inside of her, she smiled, rubbing her belly.

"Those 'things', as you called them, are my children. The Children of the Deep. They are simply in our true form." The words seemed to take an eternity to be deciphered by my brain, but when they were, I knew I was finished. I must have looked frightened, or confused, most likely both, and she seized the moment to demonstrate what she meant. With a rush of air, her eyes went from that crystal green to deep red, her flesh transformed from pale white to a jet-black shadow, and she hovered above me. No other facial features were distinguishable on her, but my expression must have shown it all. That, and the rapid release of my bladder.

I attempted to roll from the bed, hoping my legs would hold out long enough for me to get away from whatever demon this was. I got as far as opening the door, only to be greeted by the red-robed one. I tried to shove her out of my way, but my actions triggered a terrifying scream from all twenty or so creatures. The room was now filled with shadows of other-worldly darkness, red eyes all directed at me. They were upon me in seconds, the shadows pulling at my flesh until it tore away in strips. There were so many of them that I couldn't see what was happening, but every part of my body felt on fire, and I was beginning to lose consciousness. I heard a voice, her voice, and they backed away. I looked down at my torso, my insides now hanging out in a bloody heap. I could taste blood in my mouth, and I struggled to breathe.

She put on her previous appearance, possibly to comfort me, as she knelt by my head, stroking my hair. She looked sad, disappointed perhaps, and for a fleeting moment, I felt guilty, as if I had let her down. As if this was all my fault.

THE CONFESSIONAL

Hypocrites, every bastard one of them. That's the way I saw it anyway, and the way anyone with any sense should be able to see it. I used to think that religion had its place. I used to think that it provided a crutch for people when times became tough. That was my youthful naivety, before I really started to think about things deeply enough. The looks of condescension, from people who seemed to only live to put others down, would make my blood boil. Divorced? You're off to Hell. Had sex or, worse still, a baby out of wedlock? Off to Hell. Got a tattoo? Said a fucking swear word? Had a beer on a Saturday night? No help for you.

Perhaps it wouldn't have been so bad if the ones banging on about the rules actually obeyed them themselves. With the exception, perhaps, of monks, everyone else of a religious persuasion was more than happy to criticize others. All the while, using their religion as an excuse for their racism, homophobia, and seemingly endless wars. And that's without even starting on all the child molestation that the church so willingly covers up. Eventually, it all got too much for me to bear and I had an overwhelming desire to rid the world of the parasite that religion had become, or perhaps always had been.

This wasn't an act of rage; at least not an uncontrolled loss of temper. I was angry, yet realistic, and never believed that I could bring down religion completely. However, I could certainly do something to terrify those that treated non-believers as though they were second-class citizens. And I would make a spectacle of it, that was for sure. And now here I am, sat in this confessional booth talking to you, Father. Your precious rules prevent you from repeating my confession, don't they? And now you'll hear about everything I did in all its glory. That's okay, you stay quiet and just listen.

Four months ago, I caught my first one; it appeared fate had brought us together. You may remember seeing my work on the news? He wasn't a priest, or anything along those lines, but he helped at the local church so at least pretended to have some religious beliefs. Gerald, his name was. It came to light that his computer was filled with images of little kids, and the police stuck him on a register. Apparently too old for prison, he continued his life, minus Internet access, keeping his routine at the church. I went there one Sunday, to the church, and he was arranging the flowers. I spoke to the vicar after the service, something I struggled to stay awake through I must add, and he told me that the guy had 'repented' so all was fine. I hid my disgust as well as I could, but it must have shown on my face. I stood outside the church, watching the dirty old fucker talking to some kids, my hands balled into fists. He was to be my first.

I followed him home that day, to a small cottage on a quiet street. The front garden was well-kept, but as soon as the door opened I could smell the stench of piss and pipe tobacco. He had answered on my second knock and didn't appear to recognise me. He certainly didn't expect me to shove him on his arse and waltz into his home. He went down with a thud and I heard someone call his name. Now, this was unexpected; I'd assumed he lived alone and made a mental note to research my targets more thoroughly next time. An elderly lady poked her head around the door to what I presumed was the kitchen, her eyes suddenly widening as she saw me, and I hit her full force in the face before she could scream. She fell back, crashing into the mirror on the wall behind her and smashing it.

Gerald began to crawl towards me, his arthritic hands attempting to claw at my ankles, so I kicked him in the face and destroyed his glasses. He let out a whimper but stayed still. His wife, I don't recall her name, was sobbing and pointing into the kitchen. I think they might have had a tin of cash in there or something, as if this was a burglary! Yanking her hair back, my face an inch or two from hers, I asked her if she knew. Did you know what he had on his computer? I asked her as calmly as I could. She shook her head fiercely. I wasn't sure whether to believe her. How long have you been married? I asked. Fifty-seven years, apparently. That's a long time, wouldn't you say, Father. I'll take that grunt as a 'yes' shall I? And that's what I told her; fifty-seven years is a long time to be married to someone and not realise they are a dirty nonce. My money is on the fact that she knew, or at least had a suspicion. Maybe she was just a fucking idiot. Maybe she was stuck with him as you lot think divorce is a bigger no-no than kiddie porn. For a moment, I thought about letting her go, you know. But regardless of their ages, and putting aside whatever happy memories they may have shared, when he got caught she should have bailed on him. And that was her mistake. I picked up a piece of the broken mirror and sliced open her throat while Gerald looked on. He knew what was coming, and he knew why.

The press claimed that I stabbed him thirty-eight times, but that's nonsense. It was probably only about ten. Made a hell of a mess though. Blood poured from him, soaking the filthy carpet that he lay upon, and I watched as his eyes glazed over, a red bubble appearing from his mouth. Once I was content he was gone, I opened my bag and pulled out a can of spray paint. I sprayed the word 'pervert' a few times on the walls, changed my now rather bloody shirt, and walked out the front door, leaving it open. The press had a field day, and the general opinion was that the murders were carried out by an angry parent, or a now adult victim of Gerald. I hadn't been all that careful not to leave evidence at the crime scene, but no one saw anything, and I have no police record for fingerprints or DNA to be stored on.

How are you enjoying my story so far, Father? Still with us? Fine, don't answer, but I can hear you still breathing.

Taking another victim so near to home would have been risky. Not that I planned to get away with it in the long run, but there was still a lot of work to do. I spent the two months after Gerald scouring the Internet for another person of interest. Not wanting to limit myself to merely killing perverts, I had to expose other facets of religious oppression. Then I found the perfect opportunity; a gay rights march. Usually that kind of thing wouldn't have piqued my interest, as a straight male. Now, I'm not claiming to be some hero of gay rights; I just don't give a shit what people are into if they are honest about it, and not hurting anyone else. After all, it's your words and actions that show whether you're a decent person or not, and where you choose to consensually stick your dick has no bearing on that. Which is something the Parents Against Pride group didn't seem to understand. Perhaps they do now.

After a quick look through their Facebook group, which should certainly have been removed for hate speech, it was clear that the chief witch was strongly involved with her local religious organisation. She was the one arranging the protest against the march and, even more disturbingly, the one running the children's group to make banners for the event. It was too much to resist.

After an hours' drive, I arrived in the city which was hosting the march an hour before it was due to start. I'd seen the protesters plans online, and I was rather thrilled to find a pub opposite where they had arranged to gather. Taking a seat by the window with my pint of bitter shandy (I still had to drive back), I watched the group of about fifteen people gather, catching glimpses of their homemade signs. They were adorned with the usual homophobic slurs, I won't repeat them here, as well as the rather unoriginal 'It's Adam and Eve, not Adam and Steve'. My god, those people are idiots!

Anyway, I'll cut the story short as I doubt you have all that much time left, Father. The parade marched on, largely laughing at the bunch of protesters, who became more enraged still. Once they had had enough, they dispersed to a nearby car park and I trailed along behind them. I had no real plan, so my next move was rather bold, and I'm sure influenced by a movie. Maybe movies do promote violence, huh? Although I was already of a murderous mind so perhaps that just helped me with the ideas? Who knows? Now, the woman in question, Pamela, had come alone on that day.

Presumably her husband wanted nothing to do with it, or he had the sense to at least keep their kids away. That could be giving him too much credit; he could have been balls deep in Pamela's sister for all I knew. Whatever he was up to, it worked out well for him, and he's still alive and breathing as far as I know.

Pamela drove a car that was way too large for her petite frame; some monstrous 4x4 that she could barely see over the steering wheel in. It also turns out that she wasn't all that observant towards the back seat either, as I managed to sneak across it as soon as she pressed the unlock button, whilst she was busy exchanging nasty observations with one of her fellow Parents Against Pride. If I'd known that Pamela was heading straight home, I would have put together a better plan, but I really was winging it to begin with.

I remember lying on that leather back seat, certain that at any moment she would hear my breathing and I'd have to react quickly, but she did not. Twenty minutes later she parked up, outside what I guessed was her house. As we pulled into a space on the street, I withdrew the cheese wire from my jacket pocket. She turned off the ignition and I struck, quickly lifting it over the headrest and pulling it tight against her throat. Her legs kicked, but the more she pulled against the wire, the deeper it cut. I pulled the handles in a sawing motion, feeling the movement become easier as the wire moved below, through the skin. Even after Pamela had gone limp, I kept at it, almost decapitating her. As quietly as I could, I retrieved the same can of spray paint I had used at Gerald's, wrote 'homophobe' on the side of her car, and disappeared down a side street.

Are you still conscious? I don't hear anything; hang on, I'll come around to your side. Jesus Christ! Look at the state of you! Hello? You still in there? Well, there's a pulse so I'll just assume you can hear me. Where was I? Oh yeah, Matthew and the sanctity of marriage. I guess it's true about those who doth protest too much. This guy was real bastard. Okay, picture this: Matthew was a speaker at an evangelical church, one of those super lively places that insist on the reality of miracles and seem more popular with the youngsters. His specialty subject, the one he banged on about at any given opportunity, was marriage. And, unsurprisingly, his view of marriage was based on religious teachings. Marry once, don't get divorced, the wife is to be obedient, and so on. Not very modern, but neither is the church. As I explained, (I hope you got that), my issue is with the hypocrisy more than some outdated belief system. So, imagine my surprise when I found out that Matthew was married, not to his second wife, but his third! I did a bit of digging, and marriages one and two ended following claims of domestic violence and sexual assaults. I guess the previous wives were not as obedient as Matthew had wanted! And the third, Penny, was going through the same ordeal, she just hadn't had the courage to leave yet. But it was okay, because I would be setting her free very soon.

I paid her a visit when Matthew was at work, having knocked up a fake ID and claiming to be from the local authority. I told her we had received reports of suspected violence against her and wanted to check on her well-being. She accepted what I told her as truth, breaking down in tears almost immediately. We talked for some time that day, and I was overcome with a feeling of compassion as I listened to her problems, promising that nothing would be said until she was ready to do so. I told her about Matthew's previous wives, and she was shocked. She thought she was his first, both in marriage and in the bedroom. Penny admitted that, at times, he had been rough with her, but did not realise she had been sexually assaulted. Poor girl was so naive. She told me that sometimes she would say no, and he'd climb on anyway, but she thought that was how marriages worked; Matthew had said so. I was trying to control my anger, to appear to be the professional Penny thought I was. I gave her the phone number for the Domestic Violence Hotline and said my goodbyes. She made me promise not to tell anyone, and I agreed. Of course, I'd be telling Matthew, but he wouldn't be repeating anything.

By this time, I had developed quite a taste for the killing, and before you say anything, I know it's a bit wrong. But I never proclaimed it as a sin and then went about doing it; I'm not a hypocrite. The media had picked up on the connection between Gerald and Pamela, but my message didn't seem to be being understood. So, I ramped it up a notch with Matthew. He was a big fucker, and from what I'd discovered, he was likely to be quite handy with his fists. I can't pretend to dislike violence obviously, but I'm not all that good in a fight. This was going to be harder than bumping off a couple of pensioners and a woman. So, I drugged him. It wasn't anywhere near as difficult as you'd think. I waited by his car, which was in his workplace's car park, and when he came over, I jabbed a needle in his neck. It was only morphine, which I'd had lying around at home after some surgery a while ago, but it did the trick. I shoved him into his car, and drove away, finding a quiet spot in the countryside.

Before he came to, I bound his wrists with cable ties, kept the seatbelt on for a bit of extra protection, and pushed one of his socks into his mouth as a gag. There were no people around for miles, but I didn't want to risk him screaming. This time, I had the chance to tell him exactly why I was there. Are you wondering why *you're* in the state you are? I'm sure you know, Father. We'll get to that soon. Anyway, I had Matthew in the passenger seat of his car, hands tied, mouth gagged. He looked bloody terrified when he woke up, but I suppose that was to be expected. He lashed about as much as he could, but it wasn't any good, and once he had calmed himself a bit I started to explain.

I told him that I knew about his previous wives, that I knew how he had treated them, and was now treating Penny. You should have seen his face when I told him I'd been to see her; that was a look of real anger. He was trying to talk to me, but I didn't take the gag out. It would have been bullshit anyway and I'm sure it would have made things worse for him. You could say I did him a favour by not listening. Now, this bit is important, and something I failed to get across to Gerald and Pamela. I explained to Matthew that whilst hitting your wife, and sexually assaulting her, is a pretty fucked up thing to do, under normal circumstances I would have just reported it to the police. What brought us to this situation was his constant preaching about the sanctity of marriage. I asked if he understood and he nodded rather enthusiastically. I suppose he would have agreed with anything I'd said at that point. So, I told him that the punishment needed to fit the crime. I remember that puzzled look on his face, as I unzipped his trousers and pulled out his dick. It was only afterwards that I realised he thought I was going to sexually assault him as a form of revenge, and by the way his dick grew I don't think that would have bothered him too much.

I was pretty glad it grew so quickly, as I wasn't planning to touch it for any longer than necessary. I looked into Matthew's eyes, his dick in my hand, and felt a little awkward. I'm not sure what the look on his face was, but it quickly changed. I swapped my hand, now holding his boner in my left, reaching for the switchblade with my right. He knew what was happening as soon as he caught sight of the metal. He let out a moan, his eyes widening as I held his bloody stump of a penis up in front of his face. Blood poured from the wound, soaking the foot well in front of him, and I sat in silence waiting for him to bleed out. It took seventeen minutes. I didn't have to hurry as we were so secluded, and I took my time redecorating his car. This time I had to switch to a black paint, as Matthew drove a bloody yellow car! I mean, that is almost a reason to kill him in itself, surely? As neatly as I could manage, I sprayed the word 'rapist' on the car roof, 'wife-beater' on one side, and 'hypocrite' on the other. Then I retrieved his cock from where I had left it on the dashboard, threw it into some bushes, grabbed my bag, and began the long walk back to supposed civilization.

I spent the next few days checking the papers for any news, and when the story finally broke, one smart policeman seemed to understand my motive. Here, I have the article with me, and I'll read you a bit. *We believe, following the most recent crime scene, that the killer is targeting those he, or she, believes to be acting in a hypocritical way. All the victims have been linked to religious organizations, and all have been involved in dubious activities. Currently, it is unclear whether the perpetrator is also of a religious persuasion and trying to remove the 'bad apples' from the church, but that is a theory we are working with.*

Well, if they are looking in religious groups then they won't find me there! Ha, although I'm currently sitting in this church with you, so that's an interesting thought. However, I can't see the police raiding this place any time soon. You don't look like you've got long left, Father. And you're getting blood all over the nice wood. Did you know, I thought about crucifying you, but it seemed a bit over the top. I'm sure when they find you with your guts hanging out then that will be adequate. Right! One more confession, then I'll leave you to it. This one is yours, so you'll want to pay attention. Don't worry though, I don't expect you to say anything.

We've met before, but I doubt you remember. Well, we didn't talk to each other so it's fine, but I was at the shelter last week. The one where you were taking that donation and getting photographed by the press. It irritated me, that you could be after the praise for making a charitable donation. I'm pretty sure that's a sin, isn't it? But I haven't killed you for that. I did a bit of digging, wondering what skeletons would fall out, and you didn't disappoint. Well, you did in a way, but you didn't surprise me I should say. So far as I can tell, you aren't a nonce, so that is a big plus for you. But you are a greedy little fucker, aren't you?

You own three cars, right? That's a rhetorical question. And a pretty big house for a priest's salary. Convincing the poorest people to throw ten per cent of their money into your collection pot is one thing, if it actually goes to a good cause, but pocketing it yourself is pretty low, even for a man of the cloth. You still there? Let's see how the old pulse is going. Hmm, can't find it Father. Fuck! Guess it's bye-bye for you. You don't mind if I decorate the side of this lovely mahogany booth, do you? I was going to write 'embezzler' but we're short of space. I guess 'thief' will be fine.

Then I'll be on my way, I promise. I'm sure it won't be long before the police are knocking at my door and I have a few more people to visit. Maybe I'll start a journal, so that when I am caught I'll have the chance to get my side across. Perhaps even a bestselling novel? People love reading all that grisly stuff. I just need a title. *Don't be a fucking hypocrite!* sounds a bit shit. *Practice what you preach* is better. Ooh, *Righting their wrongs*. I like that one.

MEREDITH

Meredith O'Brien's house was a small one; a red-brick construction built to last. Nearly ninety years on, and it was almost as solid as the day it had been built. The only structural change in all this time had been to move the toilet indoors, and this had been put-off until Meredith's husband, Bill, had become too ill to trudge to the outhouse each time he felt the urge. That had merely been a decade ago, and Bill had struggled on for another four years before the prostate cancer finally took him, leaving Meredith alone. Living independently after almost sixty years of marriage took some adjustment, but Meredith found it to not be anywhere near as unpleasant as she had expected.

Of course, there was sadness, she had lost her husband, but she was not one to mope, and certainly had no intention of joining him any sooner than necessary. They had been unable to have children, and most of their friends had either moved away or been cremated by this point, and so Meredith passed her time painting, and writing the novel she had always dreamed of completing. Life was peaceful, and this was how Meredith liked things. She still found herself talking aloud, on occasion, with comments that would have been aimed at Bill, if only he could hear her. Meredith took pleasure in reading each completed chapter from her armchair, as if reading to a keen listener rather than her empty house. Life would have stayed this way too, if it wasn't for those bastard developers.

Once a week, Meredith left the house to shop for groceries, carefully planning what she would eat so as not to have to go any other days. This was always on a Friday morning, after breakfast, and before she sat down to add to her piece of fiction. The small, red-brick house was one of only four properties which had remained homes on that street; the rest gradually being renovated and marketed as retail premises. Meredith was a frugal woman and had no interest in the shops that had sprung up along her little street over the past few years. Food was a necessity, a bottle of Mother's Ruin was a treat once a month, but she needed little else.

Her lack of interest in the opening of other businesses meant that she did not notice when they began to close, either. Until, one rainy Friday morning, she couldn't get her groceries. The shop's windows were whitewashed, with no sign of life. Of course, there had been a closing down sign in all the windows for weeks before it had actually happened, but Meredith never took the time to read the signs. All that remained was a small poster displaying the address of the nearest store. The rain was becoming heavier, and Meredith could not remember the last time she had ventured farther than where she currently stood. Bewildered, she ventured to the end of the street and glanced in all directions, hoping it would not be too far to go.

An hour later, Meredith dragged her tartan shopping trolley through her front door, removed her soaking coat, and slumped into an armchair to think. She didn't like the shop she had found; it was expensive, farther away, and the people working there couldn't speak English. She scolded herself a little for her casual racism but could not deny that she found it irritating being unable to understand what the staff were saying to one another.

Unaware of any other options, Meredith resigned herself to the same journey on the following Friday. She was thankful that the weather was far more pleasant this time and made a conscious effort to take in her surroundings. She lived exactly halfway along the street. There were twelve properties for her to pass as she headed towards the junction at the end of the road. Nine businesses, including the grocery shop, all had either closed signs in the windows, whitewashed windows, or heaps of mail visible through the glass doors. There were three houses and, despite the lack of any *sold* signs on display, they looked long-since abandoned.

"This town is really going downhill," Meredith mumbled to herself, hoping the new shop would have some decent gin, and feeling desperate to get home.

Almost four weeks passed, the days filled with the usual routine, until there came a knock at the door. Three hard knocks, in fact, which caused Meredith to jump a little, and adding too much paint to the brush she was holding.

"Who on earth could that be?" she mumbled. No-one ever came to visit, there was no-one she knew well enough. Meredith's first thought was that it could be someone selling something, either tat she didn't need, or a religion that she had no interest in. In which case, it would be simpler to ignore the caller. *Surely there are too few homes along here now to justify sending out salespeople?* Meredith pondered. *Or someone needs help?* A little reluctantly, she made her way to the door and opened it, letting out an audible sigh. She was greeted by two overweight men in suits, both wearing lanyards, one holding a clipboard.

"Good afternoon Mrs. O'Brien. My name is Patrick Matthews, and this is my colleague, Daniel Smith."

"I'll stop you there," Meredith began. "I have everything I need, both physically, and spiritually."

"We're not here to sell you anything," Smith interjected. "We're following up on the letter that we sent you some months ago, regarding your house." Meredith's face was blank.

"Did you not receive our letter, Mrs. O'Brien?"

"I don't open my mail," she explained. "No-one writes to me, my bills are all paid, and everything else is junk."

"I see," Matthews said, looking a little nervous. The letter would have given some warning, but now he had to do it himself. "You have probably noticed that the other properties on this street have closed, the homes are empty?"

"I'm aware of that. I have to walk farther to get my shopping now, and I'm not happy about it."

"Sorry to hear that. We represent the firm which has purchased the properties on this street, with a view to developing the land. Due to the generous offers made, we have had no difficulty in obtaining them all. Except yours, Mrs. O'Brien." Meredith stared at the men for a moment, processing what she had heard.

"My house is not for sale, if that's what you're getting at?"

"We are aware of the market value, Mrs. O'Brien, which has dropped since the closures of the businesses around you. We are willing to offer you fifty per cent over and above that value."

"I don't care if you are offering one hundred times the value; the house is not for sale. I'm too old to be moving house now, I have enough money for myself, with no-one to leave it to if I had more. I'll be in this house until they take me out in a box." With that, Meredith closed the front door, and headed to the kitchen to fix a large gin. Her hands shook as she poured a triple measure into the tumbler, hating confrontation but angry at the audacity of the developers, and upset by the thought of her home being demolished. Despite having stated her position clearly, Meredith had a niggling suspicion that they would not give up quite so easily.

Two days had passed before Matthews and Smith returned. Meredith tried ignoring the banging at the door, but they were persistent, and she had had enough.

"I've told you I'm not selling," she stated, before either man could speak.

"We understand that, Meredith. May I call you Meredith?" Smith began.

"No, you may not," Meredith snapped back.

"Apologies. We have discussed the conversation we had last time and feel able to make you a substantially higher offer. Now, I know…" was as far as the conversation went before Smith found the door closing in his face. Instinctively, he placed a foot against the door frame, preventing it shutting completely. Meredith tried to hide the fear from her face as she took a step back, focusing on the feeling of anger instead.

"If my husband was still alive, you wouldn't get away with this behaviour! Now move your foot before I call the police!"

Matthews nodded at Smith, who slowly retracted his foot. No sooner had he moved it than the door slammed shut, seemingly of its own accord. Meredith stared at the door, trying to convince herself that, despite the stillness in the air, it had blown shut.

"Stupid woman," she heard one of them say. "Looks like it's Plan B."

Plan B? Meredith wondered. *Offer more money? Send in the heavies? Do people really do that? Well, I won't be bullied out of my home.* The return of the two men had set Meredith on edge, and she double locked the front door as a precaution against their return.

Jason sat in greasy cafe cradling his coffee as he awaited his employers. It was shady business, but he'd been doing their dirty work for years by this time, and never considered quitting. The money was good, as with most illegal employments, and he took a certain pleasure in completing each task. He glanced towards the door as the two suits walked in, taking the seats across the table from him.

"What you got for me?" Jason asked. Matthews slid a scrap of paper across the sticky table, an address written on it.

"The boss needs this place. But the owner won't sell."

"How many in the house?" Jason asked.

"Just her; Meredith O'Brien. She's old, got to be more than eighty. No interest in money, says she's too old to move. Stubborn woman."

"OK," Jason replied, downing the last mouthful of cold coffee and standing to leave.

"Whatever it takes," Matthews told him, grabbing his arm. "We need her out within the week." Jason leaned towards Matthews' face and grinned.

"Take your fucking hand off me, unless you want to lose it." Matthews withdrew his hand, keeping eye contact with Jason.

"Just do what we pay you for." And Jason was gone.

Meredith rarely looked out on the street, preferring the view of her small back garden, which her painting room provided her with. This meant that for the rest of the day, Jason could observe the house from his car without being noticed. He clocked a few lights coming on and off inside, confirming that the owner was at home. He noted in his small notebook that she did not leave the house on that day. Once it was late enough to assume that Mrs. O'Brien would be sleeping, he approached the front door and gently tried the handle. There was no room for movement and hoping that the coast was clear, he shone a torch between the door and the frame. *Double-locked. Shit.* On the left-hand side of the house ran a narrow pathway, leading to the side entrance of the building next-door. A building that had once been a home, then a Polish food shop, and now sat empty. Carefully, Jason side-stepped past three plastic wheelie bins overflowing with rubbish. To his disappointment, there was no side door, or garden entrance, to Meredith's property. There was, however, also no lighting at the back of the property, and he was completely hidden from sight. The garden was bordered by a fence, approximately six feet in height, but certainly scalable.

Keeping his torch off, Jason pulled himself over the fence and slid quietly onto the flower bed that ran the length of the garden, destroying a couple of pansies on the way. The house sat in darkness, and he could just about make out the white uPVC frame of the back door, which led from the garden into the kitchen. He tried the door, on the off chance it had been left unlocked, but no such luck. He decided to call it a night, once he had left his mark in the garden. After Jason had pulled up every flower that he could manage, kicking dirt across the lawn, he turned his attention to the ornaments, knocking them over, or simply flipping them upside-down. All the while, he could not shake the feeling that he was being watched. This kind of nocturnal, criminal activity was not something new to Jason, and there was always a little paranoia about being spotted. However, this felt different, like there were eyes on him. It was as he turned to destroy the bird bath that he was startled by something moving; a shadow in the periphery of his vision. He looked around but saw nothing. As his foot connected with the bird bath once again, the shadow seemed to swirl around him for a second before disappearing. *Bastard cat,* he thought, optimistically. Cat or no cat, Jason was sufficiently spooked to be on his way.

Meredith almost dropped her teacup when she looked out of the kitchen door on the following morning. Despite the garden being small, she kept it presentable. The grass area was kept tidy, the beds were always filled with seasonal flowers, and the ornate wooden bird table (which Bill had hand-carved himself) sat proudly in the centre. That is, until now. Huge chunks of grass and soil had been ripped from the lawn, every single flower had been yanked out by the roots and, most upsetting of all, the bird table now lay scattered in pieces. She had never experienced anything like this before and had no doubts as to who was responsible. Without hesitation, Meredith called the police, foolishly thinking that they would be able to catch the perpetrator.

"We will have a chat with the men who came by," the officer told her, with a look that said, *'Don't get your hopes up.'* "But there is a good chance this was just kids. In the meantime, keep your house secure and get in touch if anything else happens." The police gave the garden another quick look-over before making their exit, all under the watch of Jason, who was parked a few buildings down from the house.

Deciding to deal with the mess outside a little later, Meredith grabbed her shopping trolley and made her way out the front door, double locking it and trying the handle to be certain. She was visibly shaken, glancing up and down the street before she began the journey. *It has to have been those bastards,* she told herself. *Surely when the police confront them, they will back off.* From the crossroads, it was another ten-minute walk to the convenience store. She dragged her cart around, unable to concentrate on what she was really doing, not noticing the man who watched her from the end of each aisle. Once she had paid, and made her way outside, she did not notice him approach her from behind until he was inches from her face.

"You really should think about moving," he said with a grin. "At your age, people tend to have a lot of falls." Before she could reply, Jason was running ahead of her, disappearing out of sight. Meredith froze, attempting to process the threat she had received, unsure of what to do. However, it wasn't fear that she felt, as much as anger. *The police will have to act now!*

Meredith's pace quickened, as she hurried home to call the police. The fear that this unpleasant man could be waiting for her loitered at the back of her mind, but the idea of heading straight to the police station didn't occur to her. Reaching the door to her home, Meredith fumbled inside her handbag trying to locate her keys.
"For goodness' sake!" she muttered, slowly removing each item in her search. As she took out the last objects, a look of horror spread across her face as she realised that they were not there. She knew full well that she had needed to use them to lock her front door, and the chance of them simply falling from her bag was virtually zero. Cautiously, Meredith tried the door, half expecting it to be unlocked and her assailant waiting within. However, the door remained firmly closed, with no way for her to gain entry.
For ten minutes, Meredith stood outside of her own home, weighing up her options, trying to hold back the tears that were forming. Taking the walk to the police station was her only choice now, but before she had taken a step, a car pulled up beside her.
"Having some difficulties, Mrs. O'Brien?" Matthews shouted through the open car window, barely concealing the smug look on his face. Meredith reacted before thinking, anger taking hold, and she marched towards the car, swinging her now empty handbag at the man. Her attack

was met with laughter. "Calm down, love. This is all going to be fine." Matthews reached into his jacket pocket and passed Meredith a folded piece of paper. She opened it, staring incredulously at the cheque. It was a large sum of money, but she had no intention of accepting it and tore it to pieces in front of him, scattering the pieces in the breeze.

"I'm going to the police. You've effectively stolen my home."

Matthews feigned a worried look.

"Fine. You can have your keys back. We give up." He handed the bunch of keys over, which Jason had passed to him at the far end of the road. Meredith snatched them away from him, scuttling inside without noticing that there was one missing.

Meredith tried to predict how the police would act. After all, she had her keys back, and these bastards had, albeit unconvincingly, said they were giving up on their attempts to buy her home. *I should report it anyway; at least get it on record somewhere in case they return.*

"We'll get an officer out to see you, Mrs. O'Brien, but it may not be until tomorrow, I'm afraid." This wasn't the news that Meredith wanted to hear, but she remained polite and thanked the switchboard operator. She had rolled her eyes when advised to keep the doors and windows locked, trying to resist making a sarcastic comment about how she had planned to leave everything open for anyone to wander in. With a hot cup of tea, Meredith sat herself in the armchair and thought over the events of the day.

"They wouldn't dare to do this if you were still here Bill," she said aloud, her eyes falling on their wedding photograph, which sat on the mantel piece. "You'd take care of everything." Meredith could feel her eyes moisten, as she fought back tears. "Why did you have to leave?" she said, a hint of anger evident. A gust of wind caused the curtains to flap, startling Meredith. Certain the windows had been closed, she stood up, to find that they still were. She looked around the room in confusion, teacup still in hand. Meredith let out a yelp as the small cupboard door in the corner of the living room swung open. Transfixed she stood, rooted to the spot, as two scenic jigsaw puzzles appeared to fall from the space, followed by a very old Scrabble set. Then nothing.

After a good ten minutes of not knowing how to react, Meredith put the events down to something explainable, despite the fact she could not fathom what. Only as she went to place the items back in the cupboard did she feel it, feel him, gently touching her arm. She flinched at the cold touch, but the familiarity of it was undeniable.

"Bill?" she whispered, trembling, and feeling a little silly for even thinking he could still be around. The Scrabble set moved. Meredith cautiously bent down to pick it up, but an unseen force knocked it from her hands, scattering the lettered tiles across the carpet. Feeling faint, Meredith sat back in her chair, staring at the floor as the tiles began to move.

First an 'I' took its place in front of her, at her feet, before being joined by more letters. Meredith's eyes widened as the words formed; I didn't leave, Merry. No-one but Bill had called her Merry, not ever. She had no doubt that he was there, but the shock was enough for her pass out where she sat.

By the time she regained consciousness, more letters had been added, telling Meredith that Bill loved her. She watched as they shifted back and forth, unseen hands spelling out the words that he would keep her safe when those men returned. However, Meredith didn't care anymore. Having never been particularly religious, she hadn't expected there to be anything beyond the earthly life. Now she had no doubts that they could reunite in death, and she wanted nothing more than to join her husband.

"I want to come with you," she told him. "They can have the damned house." The tiles moved, more slowly this time as if Bill was unsure how to respond. 'Not yet', Meredith read, followed by 'not because of them'. She began to sob. "I'm ready, Bill. You have no idea how lonely I've been! What do you want me to do? Keep living alone, our conversations reliant on bloody Scrabble tiles?!" There was a pause, much longer than Meredith expected, as Bill was clearly thinking through their options. The tiles shifted purposefully. 'Revenge first'.

Bill was angry, that much was clear to Meredith. The threat she was facing had, through an unexpected series of events, caused her to want to die. The developers had essentially killed Meredith, whether it had been their intention or not. The tiles jumped about on the rug. 'Call them'. Meredith pondered Bill's intentions, doubting that inviting those men to the house would end well for them. "I can't," Meredith began.

Before she could speak again, a clatter from the kitchen startled her. Curtains and papers rustled in the living room as Bill moved about. She could swear she saw a shadow leave the room and head towards the kitchen. Hands trembling, heart racing, Meredith followed and found Jason stood in her kitchen.

"What the hell are you doing in my house?" Meredith demanded, trying to hide her fear. "I'm calling the police!" Jason lunged towards the elderly woman, grabbing her by the forearm and turning her back to face him.

"I'm only doing my job, lady. You'd be much better off just selling the house." Jason couldn't read the expression on Meredith's face, a mixture of fear and surprise, followed by a smirk of satisfaction. If he had seen what came from behind him, Jason would have understood, but the first thing he noticed was the warm sensation in the side of his neck. Jason's grip on Meredith eased a little as he raised his free hand up to the now wet area. Dabbing his fingers in the moisture, he examined his hand to see the unmistakable crimson of his own blood. He placed a hand on the kitchen counter to steady himself, as dizziness took hold. Jason did his best to see who was behind him, but the knife struck again, plunging into his side repeatedly until he gurgled his final breath, drenched in red from head to toe.

Meredith stared as her kitchen knife etched words into the wooden countertop. 'Call them.' She was afraid, not only of the men who wanted her gone from her home, but now of Bill. Such a level of violence was out of character for him, certainly whilst he had been alive, but death brings a greater degree of freedom. Attempting to keep her voice level, Meredith retrieved the crumpled letter from her wastepaper bin, and dialled the number.

"Mr. Matthews?" she began. "Meredith O'Brien." There was a moment of hesitation. *Probably wondering if his thug has been here yet,* Meredith thought.

"Mrs. O'Brien, what a lovely surprise. What can I do for you?"

"I wish to sell the house. But it needs to be tonight."

"Well, I can't pretend to not be happy about that. What brought on the sudden change of heart?" Matthews asked, unsure if he really wanted to know.

"I'm sure you can guess, Mr. Matthews. I'm too old for all this nonsense, and as much as I think that you, and your firm, are the lowest of all God's creatures, I'm not going to stay here worrying about what you'll do next. Bring your cheque book and a contract round, and let's get this over with." With that, Meredith hung up the receiver and returned to the kitchen. Gingerly stepping over the body on her linoleum flooring, taking care not to slip on the ever-increasing blood puddle, Meredith poured a large gin into one of her crystal tumblers. "The ball's in your court now, Bill," she said aloud.

Barely fifteen minutes later came a knock at the door, and Meredith was greeted by Mr. Matthews.

"Come in," she said, trying to hide her disappointment that he had come alone. "Your partner couldn't make it?"

"I didn't think it was necessary to drag him out; I'll call him when we are done. Where would you like me?"

"Living room," Meredith replied, nodding her head towards the nearest door. She followed him in, taking her position in the armchair, whilst he sat across the room from her.

"It's a pretty standard contract," he began. "It states that you are happy to transfer the deeds for the property over to the development firm, at the price stated within. The only parts which need completing are your signature, and the date at which the transfer would take place. How soon are you able to move?"

"Tomorrow," she told him. His eyes registered surprise, but he certainly looked pleased that it could be so soon. "And I would like the cheque made out to the local hospital. They took care of my husband before he passed, so it seems like the right thing to do."

"The whole amount?" the man asked, a little uncertain. "Do you not need some for the purchase of another property?"

"Do you want to buy the bloody house or not? What business is it of yours what I do with my money?" Meredith fixed him with a glare, and he said no more, reaching into his case for the cheque book and a pen. Meredith folded the payment in half, sliding it into her blouse pocket, before signing the contract.

"Well, that wasn't too painless, was it?" Matthews said, a little smugly.

"Not yet," Meredith mumbled. Matthews stood to leave, the contract still firmly in his hands. "Oh, one more thing. Have you met my husband, Bill?" A puzzled look spread over his face. *Old bat's gone a bit senile,* he thought.

"Er, I thought you said your husband had died, Mrs. O'Brien?"

"Yes, he is dead, that's correct. Nevertheless, he'd still like to meet you." Meredith grinned at the man, who looked a little flustered. Before he could take a step, the curtains flapped again. Matthews managed to get as far as the doorway of the living room before being launched backwards by an unseen force, hitting his head against the fireplace.

"What the fuck?" he mumbled, looking up at Meredith. Matthews felt a weight on his chest, keeping him to the ground. He screamed for help, unable to understand his predicament.

"Screaming won't help, I'm afraid. All the buildings around here are empty, remember?" Meredith looked content as she watched on from her armchair. The fireplace had not been used for decades, but it was ornamental, complete with an antique basket containing a brush, shovel, tongs, and poker. Meredith watched as the poker appeared to float in mid-air, before slamming down into the wooden floorboard, piercing Matthews' hand and securing him to the spot. He let out another scream, but it became muffled as the tongs entered his mouth, snapping at his tongue. They were blunt, but Bill's ghostly grip was tight, and the gurgling sound which accompanied the spurt of blood signified the loss of Mr. Matthews' tongue. There was only a soft moan, as the poker was ripped back through the man's hand and appeared to be aimed at his genitals.

"There's no need for that!" Meredith scalded her husband. "Just get it over with, please." The poker moved quickly, aligning itself with Matthews' face, specifically above his left eye. He tried to wriggle his head away from under the weapon but could not get it to move far enough. Meredith watched as the front of Mr. Matthews' navy-blue suit trousers darkened with urine, only seconds before Bill dealt his death-blow. As quick as an arrow, the poker forced its way through eye and brain with a squelch. His right leg twitched momentarily, then all was still.

"I need to find a stamp," Meredith explained, rising from her chair, cheque in hand. The rather large payment was quickly sealed into an envelope, addressed, and stamped. "I'm going to post this, then I'll be back," she told Bill. The street was silent, to her relief, and she made her way to the end of the road as quickly as possible, where the nearest post box stood. The redness of the box reminded her of the scene inside her home, and for a brief moment she felt something similar to regret. *Too late now,* she told herself, knowing there was only one way in which this could end. Letting herself back through the front door, and removing her coat, Meredith took to her armchair for what she knew would be the last time.

"So, Bill, how do we do this?" No answer. The tiles remained still on the floor. "Don't wimp out on me now Bill, I thought you were going to do this?" Meredith sat upright, eyes glistening with tears as she wondered if she could go through with suicide. "Bill!" she pleaded, letting tears fall. A cushion rose from the chair that had recently been Matthews' resting pace and moved towards Meredith. She smiled, whispering a 'thank-you'. As she closed her eyes, feeling the soft fabric press against her face, she did not try to fight it. Her chest began to sting as her lungs failed to fill, her head feeling lighter, until she was no more.

Moments passed before she could see again, but now everything had a vibrant tone to it. She gazed into Bill's eyes as he dropped the cushion and kissed her fully. "Merry, my darling. I've missed you more than words could ever convey."

"And I, you William. But you never have to miss me again."

UNEARTHED

It was dark when I opened my eyes. Darker than I expected. I waited for them to adjust a little, patiently allowing them to observe the familiar shadows within my bedroom, but they did not. I kept still, only my eyes darting around. For the briefest of moments, I thought I had lost my sight, until the light on my watch-face told me otherwise. 1.47am. It was too dark. I reached for the duvet but was unable to find it. I turned onto my side, sliding a hand across to feel for my lover; it did not find her, instead striking something hard and rough. Without taking a moment to think, I rolled onto my back, reaching out to the other side; to what should have been the edge of the bed. Again, a hard, rough surface met my fingertips. Now I was awake. I tried to sit up quickly, unable to see the same rough surface barely six inches above me, and grazed my forehead in the process. Fear had dilated my pupils, but the darkness remained impenetrable. I pressed the light on my watch, its meagre glow providing little assistance. Tentatively, I reached behind me to find the same surface. I slid down to what should have been the foot of my bed, my heels striking the end of my coffin. For this was surely where I was, entombed in wood. Without any cover the chill was noticeable, even on this summer night. My hands found their way down my side, confirming that I remained as I had gone to bed - naked.

Considering my circumstances, I had remained calm thus far, assessing my situation with deliberate thought. Nevertheless, try as I might, I could not recall anything that had led me to this place. We had gone to bed at around the same time as always, made love in the way that we usually did, and had fallen asleep. That was barely two hours ago. *Nothing suspicious, or out of the ordinary, had happened that evening, had it?* I racked my brain, trying to recall something which could constitute a clue, but came up with nothing. *Idiot! Perhaps trying to get out of here should be a priority?* I could have been anywhere, and the late hour drastically reduced the chances of anybody passing by, no matter my location. Air was a commodity not to be wasted, and so, against my natural impulses, I resisted the urge to scream for help. I suppose I was still in a state of disbelief, hoping this would turn out to be a prank of some kind, even though I could think of no-one who would go to such extremes. Gently, I pressed my hands against the boards to my left and right, trying to detect a weakness, but found none. I had enough space to roll over, but not enough room to get my head to where my feet currently were. Knowing that my legs were far stronger than my arms, logic told me to kick at that end, and so I did.

It felt like my only option, and I went at it hard, certain that my life may well depend on it. I cursed myself to refusing to wear bed socks, as the soles of my feet took in splinters and turned slippery with blood. Again, and again, I kicked with as much force as I could. The wood cracked eventually, but it was of little consequence. I remained unable to push the boards outward against the weight of the soil. My hope that I was merely nailed into a box disappeared as soon as I felt the damp earth on my toes and I knew, without doubt, that I was buried. If I was to escape then I would need to turn around, to be able to at least try to shovel the dirt with my hands. Six feet of wet mud would weigh a lot, I assumed, and I saw a good chance that I would be crushed under this weight. *It's either that or just wait to die. I have to find a way to turn myself around.*

The width of the box was greater than the height, so it made sense to try to turn that way, in a kind of forward roll manoeuvre. Tucking my knees up to my stomach as tightly as I could, I began to swivel my body around. My nakedness offered me no protection from the rough wood which tore against my right side. As soon as my head hit one wall, I doubted it would be possible to get all the way around; certainly not without causing some serious damage to myself. Regret came flooding in as I thought about how I had neglected my body, cursing this ring of fat around my waist. Pulling my knees in with all the strength I could muster, I let out a yelp as the soles of my feet made contact with the left side of the box, forcing my scalp to push against the right. I was wedged there, rough surfaces at both extremities, tears welling in my eyes.

I breathed deeply, preparing for what I knew was going to be almost unbearable, and dragged my feet behind me. I could feel them slicing open, but the lubrication of the blood made movement easier. As my feet moved, so did my head, sending a searing pain shooting across my scalp as I broke forth, now face-down, my head at the opening that my feet had made. Gently, I touched two fingers on to the top of my head; it felt wet and I was sure that I had left hair behind, matted into the wood. My head hurt more than my feet, but my hands were still intact, and they were what I needed now. *Dig!* I told myself. *It's the only choice.* I fumbled in the dark with my hands, beginning to pull the dirt into the box. It moved easily but was wet and heavy. I felt things crawling between my fingers; the creatures that dwell in the darkness.

The earth did not fall in on me and, one handful at a time, I managed to move it. Trying as hard as I could to ignore the pain, I shovelled lumps one by one into the box, filling the space I left behind me. Only once did I stop, tempted to give in to the exhaustion, beginning to doubt which way was up and which was down. I checked my watch; it had been almost an hour since I had awoken. I had no idea how long I would have sufficient oxygen for, but I guessed it wouldn't be much longer. My breaths were coming harder and faster. I pulled at the dirt above me once more, one scoop, two scoops, then I hit something. It felt hard, yet movable; a root perhaps. The hope that I was nearing the surface propelled me on, until my eyes detected a glimmer of light peering through the split soil. It was the top, and I was going to make it.

I pushed a hand through, feeling the cold air hit it. My other hand quickly followed, both of them frantically pulling open a large enough space for my head to fit through. Fresh air rushed into my oxygen-starved lungs, my eyes adjusted to the moonlight, and I laughed. I was in agony, not just in my scalp and my feet, but my entire, naked, body had been scraped and scratched during my ascent. *It will heal, I just need to get home.* Using the last of my strength, I pushed against my mangled feet to climb out of what was almost my tomb, and lay face-down, unclothed in the wet grass.

"Holy shit!" I heard, barely able to move my head. *Help is here. I'm going to be OK.*

"He's fucking climbed out!" came a second voice. My brain took a split-second to process what I had heard. *He's climbed out. They knew I was down there. That voice is familiar.* I began to roll over, trying to see who was there. A man whom I did not recognize stood over me, looking me up and down.

"All that for nothing," he said, almost admiringly. He turned to face someone else. "I'll take care of it."

The pain that the rest of my body felt made the attack feel almost numb; I saw a glint of steel in the moonlight, and then I couldn't catch my breath. My chest began to feel warm and sticky, as my opened throat gushed red across it. I couldn't process what was happening, or why, I just knew it was over. I looked away from my killer, turning my gaze in the direction of the familiar voice and saw her. I'd hoped she was safely still in our bed, but that was not the case. She watched the life drain out of me, no sign of remorse on her pretty face, and I was gone before I could even guess at her motivation.

WASH AWAY YOUR SINS

"What the holy fuck has happened here?" P.C. Smith asked, yanking up the garage door. The stench of blood and piss was overwhelming. His colleague, P.C. Hawkins gave the scene a quick look around, before vomiting on the floor. They had been responding to a call about what was only described as strange noises coming from the garage. Smith had assumed some kids had broken in and were drinking, or getting high, and hadn't hurried along to the scene.

"Guess we should have got here a bit quicker," Hawkins said.

"Keep that thought to yourself," Smith responded, giving his partner a stern look. He pulled the radio from his belt and called for backup.

Shortly, the garage was swarming with police.

"Boss," one of the P.C.s called out, directed at the lead detective. "You should take a look at this." He handed her a couple of sheets of paper. "Seems to be a confession, or something." The D.C.I. snatched the papers and headed outside to smoke whilst she read them.

If you are reading this, then I finally put my plan into action. There will, no doubt, be a lot of speculation as to what took place, and why have done the things I have done, so here is my attempt to explain. I knew this day was coming; it had been on the cards for some time. For years, I had wondered what event would cause me to finally snap, pondering who would push me over the edge. My anxiety had worsened over the last few years, to the point that I dreaded each new day, fearful of phone calls, emails, even what came through the post. I became a recluse, only leaving the house when absolutely necessary, terrified of human interaction.

For months, I tried to convince myself that things weren't as bad as they seemed, that I simply felt this way due to a fear of abandonment, and what the doctors had called high-functioning anxiety. Nevertheless, just because you're paranoid, doesn't mean they aren't after you. It's very hard to say if the way I have been treated by people has made me feel this way, or the way I feel has made them treat me badly. Either way, the day has finally arrived.

Since my teenage years, I had no doubt that when I did leave this world, it would be at my own hands. I have always been OK with this fact. The overbearing sense of loss as I watched my family disown me, and partners leave me, brought me close to the end on numerous occasions. However, something else is there now, something more than sadness and feelings of inadequacy. Anger has found a place, and if I'm going to make the great escape, I'm not going to go alone.

For the last three weeks, I have been plotting and scheming something elaborate, a revenge that would shock all who read about it. The idea came about after I had received a string of abusive text messages; I have left my phone unlocked at what is now certainly a crime scene, so that this can be verified. I came close to ending my life that day, slicing at my arms and legs with a scalpel after finishing almost a litre of whiskey. I broke down, seeing my own weakness for what it was, and felt overcome with a basic human need for revenge. We may now live in a supposedly civilised society, but in older times it was reasonable to strike down one's enemies. In this, I had a certain advantage; I had no intention of getting away with murder.

These past weeks have felt as though I were on autopilot, putting together the events which, if all went to plan, culminated in the bloodbath that you have discovered. I wondered several times if I was a psychopath, thoughts of torture filling my mind, but realised that I am not. I knew I would find the actions difficult, but saw them as necessary, and a punishment fitting the crime.

I began by writing down the names of those who had wronged me, even in the slightest of ways. It wasn't as long a list as I had expected, and I thought very carefully about the actions of each person when I had reduced the list to the final three. As you will see from my phone, I contacted each person with a detailed explanation as to how I felt, giving them the opportunity for reconciliation. One chose not to reply, two only made things worse for themselves.

Two of my targets, for I refuse to call them victims, lived alone so were easier to secure than the third. Toxicology reports may still show signs of Rohypnol in their systems, but I doubt that the puncture wound from the hypodermic needle will still be evident. It is easy enough to obtain drugs and the necessary paraphernalia on the streets of this dirty town, and I simply knocked on each person's door, struck out with the needle, and loaded them into my car. They weren't small men, but I was strong, physically, at least. I was fast, and under the cover of darkness, no-one suspected a thing.

The third was harder, but not by much. I suppose it was fortunate that they all knew each other, so a simple text message requesting some company was enough to draw her out after dark and into my waiting arms. She should have stayed with her family, she should have put them first instead of running to, what she thought, was a more exciting choice. But some people are just shit.

The Internet provided conflicting information as to how much Rohypnol to use, so I went higher than the maximum suggested dose. If they were to wake up early, the consequences could have been far worse than if I had accidentally killed them prematurely. As a result, it took several hours for the men to regain consciousness, and another two for her to awaken.

If this was a movie, then I'm sure I would have built an elaborate kill room in some disused warehouse, but these places simply do not exist around here. The only places available to me were my own home, and the garage that I rent several streets away. As you will know by now, I opted for the garage as it is a little more secluded. Further from other people, but hardly soundproof.

As soon as the first started to stir, I was on him, scalpel in hand, and took his tongue. I gagged a little at the feel of the wetness, frightened it may slip into his throat and cause him to choke. The benefit of rendering him silent was two-fold, not only was he unable to scream for help, he also had no way to try to talk me out of what I was going to do. I had my doubts as to whether or not I could go through with it if someone began pleading for their life.

For two hours I sat in that garage in silence, the two men bound with rope, wide-eyed and tongueless, staring back at me with a look of terror, and something else. Regret perhaps? As if they knew why they were there. One tried to move about, a strange grunting sound all he could manage, but I struck his hand with a hammer, and he became still. When she started to murmur, I repeated the procedure, slinging her tongue rather unceremoniously on the garage floor with the others.

Once she calmed down a little, which I'm sure was difficult under the circumstances, I began to explain. This is the part I had been looking forward to; a chance to say how I felt, how I had been wronged, without them being able to argue back or walk away. And so, I did. I reminded each of them how they had lied about me, how they had tried in every way imaginable to destroy my life, how they had made me feel. Their fate was apparent to them now, and their expressions appeared to alternate between defiant, remorseful, and confused. But I had said my piece, and it felt as though a weight had been lifted. In fact, I almost considered releasing them at this point. Almost.

On the drunken nights leading up to this moment, I had watched the most extreme horror films that I could find, wondering at the possibilities of using such extravagant torture methods. As I had felt queasy about the tongue removal procedure, I was now glad to have not gone for anything so gory when the time came. I needed something symbolic about the way their lives would end, and as most of their criticism of me had been based on their bizarrely interpreted religious beliefs, it seemed that my own version of holy water would be appropriate. If there really was such a thing as holy water, I have no doubt it would have scorched their flesh when exposed to it, due to the hypocritical ways they had lived their lives. However, in the real world, I would have to settle for acid. Hydrofluoric acid works well in TV shows at dissolving organic matter, but sodium hydroxide is the most practical. It is easily made at home with household equipment and can be stored in plastic bottles. I have some chemistry knowledge but was thankful to find instructional videos online.

I created enough sodium hydroxide to fill a plastic container, keeping it as concentrated as I could, and found myself holding the bottle as I looked down on my enemies. All I had really wanted was for them to love me, but they had pushed me to this. And now it was time for their god to save them, if he could. I explained my intentions, as clearly as I could, all the while watching the fear spread across their faces as the tears streamed down. I told them I held a bottle of sodium hydroxide, that if they were decent people, their god would protect them from its ferocity. I reminded them how they had brought me down in the name of religion, and that if they had been in the right, they would be perfectly safe and free to go. I suppose it was me looking for evidence as well, some proof of a higher power. Of course, I was more than aware that if their god chose to save them at that point, it would also validate the way they had treated me, proving I was nothing but a worthless creature undeserving of love.

I approached the first and, with rubber glove encased hands, I opened the bottle. He scrunched his face up in anticipation of the impending attack, perhaps hoping that the pain would be survivable. It would have been a mistake to think that. I poured around a third of the bottle onto his short, greying hair, and my holy water hissed on contact.

He made strange noises from his throat as the acid dissolved a way through his hair, through his scalp and bubbled away on his now-exposed skull. It must have been excruciating, but the acid was not strong enough to find a way through the bone and end his suffering. The others had turned away, unable to watch the suffering of one they actually cared about. I was sure they would have enjoyed watching if I had been the one in pain, even before my actions today. I peered down to inspect the top of the skull, hoping the reaction had merely been slowed, but there was no sign of my 'blessing' progressing on. Deciding that he had suffered enough, I picked up my hammer and landed three hard blows to the exposed bone, forcing shattered pieces to puncture the grey softness beneath, and ending his life.

Breathing heavily, the two captives stared at me, pleadingly, yet seeming to know their fates were sealed. They were to go the same way, almost. I wondered if the acid had lost some of its strength dissolving the hair and decided to take a slightly different approach. Unzipping the back hold-all that I had brought along, aware that it looked exactly like a serial killer's tool kit, I pulled out the large kitchen knife. Originally, I hadn't intended to use it, but I felt safer having it available. I took hold of her ponytail, pulling her hair back as firmly as I could, before slicing the skin from the top of her head and throwing the bloody lump of skin and hair to the floor. She passed out from the pain. I poured a generous amount of the acid onto the skull to weaken it, and dispensed of her with my hammer, just as before.

Two down, one to go, and I had no issue with prolonging the final kill. I had no attachment to my last target; he was a bully, and an all-round unpleasant person. The fact that the others seemed to adore him so much, rather than me, only made me hate him more. I thought carefully about his actions, which largely involved spreading horrific lies about me, both verbally and in writing. I already had his tongue, so his hands were next. With the hammer, I broke each finger until it was a bloody pulp, and he just watched. Whatever I did, he made no sound, didn't try to move, and seemed to be accepting his fate. I remember smiling sadly at him, as I decided to get this over with.

I took his eyes next, prising them out with the blade of the kitchen knife, and adding them to the pile of gore I was building. I slumped to the floor beside him, stroking his hair as I poured the remaining acid into the holes where his eyes had recently been. He twitched a few times, and then was still; I suppose that was a relatively quick way to go.

Now you know everything, in all its brutality, so the police investigating this scene will have an easier job to do. I can only apologise to whoever has to clear up the mess, but that is something I can no longer do anything about. As you may have guessed by now, the fourth body you will have discovered is mine. I opted for the gentler approach and have taken an overdose. However this story is spun, if it makes it into the media, is of no consequence to me, but I do hope people will think about my actions, and maybe even treat each other a little more humanely.

Jesus Christ! She thought, extinguishing her cigarette. *At least it's an open-and-shut case.*

"Boss!" she heard someone shout, from inside the garage.

"What is it?"

"This guy, with the empty pill bottle. He's not dead."

Thank you for taking the time to read these stories. If you wouldn't mind taking a moment to leave a quick review on whichever site you purchased from, that would be hugely appreciated.

KEEP UP TO DATE!

More information about the author can be found on his website as well as social media profiles listed below. You can also subscribe to the email mailing list via the website for exciting news about future releases, as well as accessing short stories direct to your mailbox! If you have any comments or would like to just get in touch feel free to email directly at the address below. Happy reading!

Twitter: www.twitter.com/pjbn_author
Facebook: www.facebook.com/pjbnauthor
Instagram: www.instagram.com/pjbn_author
Web: www.redcapepublishing.com/book-shop
Email: redcapepublishing@outlook.com

Printed in Great Britain
by Amazon